Sarah's Page

by

Anna Murray

www.sarahspage.com

Sleeping Bear Press
121 South Main Street
P.O. Box 20
Chelsea, MI 48118
www.sleepingbearpress.com

Cover illustration by Barbara J. Hranilovich

Printed and bound in the United States
10 9 8 7 6 5 4 3 2 1

Cataloging-in-Publication Data
On file

ISBN 1-886947-58-9

✉ To: readers@theworld.com
From: anna@sarahspage.com
Re: Sarah's Page

It's a rough summer in Michigan for Sarah, a New York kid:

"It looked like my arm had been sucked into a printing press or something because my shirt was totally soaked with blood. So I'm thinking we're going to walk in there and they're going to move into ACTION—doctors running around, hooking me up to monitors, wheeling me away at a dead run.

But NO. I walk in there soaked with blood and they sit us down at this nice registering station and start in with a million questions. They ask Amy to produce a million plastic cards and to fill out a million forms. And I'm thinking what do I have to DO to get SERVICE around here? I swear to GOD, both my eyeballs could have dropped from their sockets and fallen SPLAT on the paperwork and that nurse would have set them aside and continued with the forms.

I can only IMAGINE what it's like to go into a hospital like Montefiore in the Bronx because they must see the most ghastly stuff all the time and not think ANYTHING is an emergency. Too bad if you've got a bone sticking out of your leg. First we've got to help this guy who walked in holding HIS BRAIN in both hands."

After a summer full of disasters and great adventures—all told in e-mail to her best friend Kate and on her web site www.sarahspage.com—Sarah grows in ways she never expected. She learns that home is all around her and travels with her, just like the Internet she loves.

Anna Murray
anna@sarahspage.com

Dedication

To my husband Jim,
who believed.

🖙 To: katie@dundee.net
From: sarah@sarahspage.com
Date: 6-15
Subject: Hurricanes, Parental Stress & Other Summer
            Activities

Dear Katie,

I know. I'm SORRY. I, like, dropped off the planet. At home every time I tried to e-mail you, Mom'd get this really CONCERNED look on her face — like little electrons were leaping off the screen and searing through my eyeballs into my brain. There's so much to tell you. Things have been REALLY whacked-out, what with leaving New York and getting shipped out HERE and all. At least I have my laptop and Mom isn't around to be an e-Nazi any more.

HERE is, of course, the state of MICHIGAN, vacationland to the stars (NOT). The fact that Michigan has phone lines and Internet access is about the only thing it has going for it. :-) You would not BELIEVE the room I am sitting in. The carpet is the color of Barney the Dinosaur. I can't believe the rental units did this to me. Especially since I have to live with my sister, Amy, and Jeff, and you know how my mom freaked out about THAT whole relationship. She swears Amy eloped just to cheat her out of a big wedding. And Mom doesn't even KNOW about the horrendous decorating. It was going to be SUCH a fun summer at the beach — until everything happened.

Before I even get too deep into explaining anything, I want to tell you that I've created my own Web site. I think after you read the rest of this e-mail, you'll realize why. It's more or less to preserve things and keep a running journal. Somehow, just writing things down the way I used to doesn't seem like enough. Not when my whole world's been turned into hummus. I think you'll really like it. Check it out at http://www.sarahspage.com.

So I guess by now I should stop avoiding the topic and bring you up to date. I'll entitle this story "How My Mother Sent Her Precious Baby Daughter to Live with Her Sister on the Prairie." Catchy? Think? The short answer is my mother couldn't deal with me anymore. The long answer may take several e-mails, but I'll do my best to get the hurricane part out of the way in this e-mail.

I guess what happened was that freaked-out spring hurricane was supposed to miss Long Island. But then it took this wild left turn in the middle of the night. This is the part where I get sad because you never saw our beach house. :-(This was supposed to be the summer you came to visit. Like, think you're FINALLY old enough to stop going to camp? Obviously my plans experienced a meltdown.

On sarahspage, I've uploaded pictures of the house. Actually it's kind of weird designing the site because it is, after all, the WORLD WIDE Web. You can't be sure that people who visit the site are from New York, like us, or even know where Southampton is. They could be from OREGON for all I know. Not that a lot of kids from Oregon are going to be logging onto my stupid little site, but you get what I mean. Anyway, it was kind of cool describing my life for someone who doesn't know anything about me. I've got maps and pictures and all kinds of stuff. I included a sample at the end of this e-mail because it'll give you a feeling of what I'm doing on the site, and who knows, maybe you have a cousin from Oregon.

Now for the blood and gore:

The hurricane wasn't SUPPOSED to hit us, according to Channel 2's weatherman Storm Field with his shiny patent-leather hair. But when did a hurricane — especially one with a politically correct name like Arethra — ever listen to Storm Field? About 2 a.m., Arethra took a hard left and slammed right into the South Shore. I know you've read all the newspaper stories. Like 10 people on our street lost their houses. :-/

I woke up hearing the roar. I had my laptop all packed. I always do if there is the least little chance of a hurricane. I can't bear the thought of leaving my data behind as my hysterical mother drags me out the door to flee to higher ground. So I grabbed the machine and ran downstairs.

The bay window was blown out. The briny water lapped at the Persian rug under my feet. My mother was standing in the middle of the living room in her bright pink-and-green Lanz nightgown and bathrobe, shouting over the surf — something about a Q'ing Dynasty vase. Dad was already in full gear. Uncle Jim was there, too. He had heard the 11 o'clock news about Arethra's hard left and called my dad from the car phone. He and my two cousins raced out to Southampton. They got to the house and everyone started hauling furniture to the old stable building in the caretaker's beat-up old truck.

The first thing I did was put my laptop under the driver's seat of my dad's Mercedes. I knew THAT car would make it out of the hurricane if my dad had to strap life preservers to it and SWIM it back to Manhattan. Back inside, Dad had one end of the Louis XVI sofa and my cousin Drew had the other. Uncle Jim was driving them like a cattle rancher. My mother was now shouting something about the Waterford crystal, which was trembling in the cabinet. Dad and Uncle Jim were focusing on BIG valuables. "Emily!" Uncle Jim yelled. "Cut that out and grab the Gosh DARN couch."

You'd think it would only take seconds for a house to go into the ocean — like those building demolition shots you see on a slow news night. You'd think that, and you'd be WRONG. It really took several hours.

As dawn was breaking, we stood on the beach. Nearly half the house was gone. It was like looking into a dollhouse with the door open. Only, the dollhouse frame was the mangled interior walls of what used to be our house. Twisted pipes and wires and chunks of concrete spilled out and away from the house. It was, as the insurance guy put it, "a total loss."

It's strange and somehow awesome to watch a whole world disintegrate. We were frozen into stone with disbelief. And yet, the weirdest part is that everyone KNEW, one day, it was coming. For YEARS we've been watching the hurricanes come in. Remember that one year the National Guard made us evacuate, but the most we got was a strong breeze? All these houses are worth a ba-jillion dollars and they're RIGHT on the dunes. And NO ONE thinks anything of it.

Do you know that, like 50 years ago, they started to predict that the south shore of Long Island was going to be totally toast by the year 2000? All these meteorologists and other geeks took a look at some data and said, "Yup. That puppy's going out with the tide. So if you rich people want to build your houses RIGHT on the water, knock yourselves out." Well, we DID knock ourselves out. My grandfather even used his political influence (he was tight with President Nixon or something) to get the Army Corps of Engineers to build these piers and tide-blocks to keep the beach from washing away. Yeah, like THAT worked. The hurricanes STILL tore down the beach, carving a whole new landscape. The day afterward you wouldn't recognize things anymore. There'd be all kinds of STUFF washed ashore. And this hill you remembered wouldn't be there anymore. Where the beach used to be wide, it was narrow. And in other places, there'd be these enormous ridges of sand that you could walk along and make forts in. So I always thought hurricanes were pretty cool. And, like my grandfather, I really kind of thought that money WOULD keep back the ocean.

But I guess I never saw a hurricane like THIS one. Who knew that our friend, humble little H_2O, is like the most destructive force in the galaxy? I've watched storms and hurricanes before and I've always been like, "MAN! That CAN'T be the same water I swam in yesterday!" But let me tell you, I've never seen ANYTHING that would compare to the ocean that night. The waves that had been warmly and gently sloshing ashore earlier in the day turned into these HUGE bear paws that heaved up, reached out onto the beach and swiped at everything in sight. And I was like, "WAIT. You're supposed to stay on the BEACH!" But instead these bear-paw waves were coming into our yard, and onto our porch and through our windows.

Station Break — I did a bunch of research on hurricanes. It's on the Web site. Check it out.

Back to our show:

Our house took the most damage on the street, though I hear the Mulholland house down the beach was a total loss as well. But everywhere you looked there was destruction. Arethra got hers from Southampton, man — in a *Bonfire of the Vanities* kind of way, if you know what I mean. You could see garages gone, cars floating over the surf. A roof, a shutter. Debris everywhere.

Speaking of floating, you would not believe all the flotsam and jetsam that came ashore in that first week after the hurricane. We were all kind of paralyzed — not knowing where to go. So we moved into a suite at the Meadow Club until my mom and dad could figure out what to do. All of the kids just kinda ended up walking the beach a lot. We'd yell back and forth to each other as we found things, "Hey, Ashley, isn't this one of your mom's sconces?"

"No, I think that's Mrs. Bostwick's."

"Eric, your dad's chess piece?"

"Some gold fixtures. Must be from the Carmichael's bathroom."

"Sarah! Like, most of this stuff is from YOUR house."

Thing is, that was true. We lost the most. I put together a box that week of scraps from my house. Things like wallpaper, a rag of silk (My mom had just had the dining room curtains done. Each window cost $1200), a pretty painted tile from the backsplash in the kitchen, broken china, a Tiffany lamp, a brass doorknocker.

I guess you can see why the Web site is so important to me. I really feel like I need it right now or I'm going to lose everything. Now, don't freak out on me. I'm not ready for Prozac — yet. It's just that memory is such a wild thing. I want to remember all there was about that house and our life because it's, like, OVER now. And I can already feel it slipping away. Especially since I'm stuck out here on the prairie. But anyway, I just want more than words. I want pictures, songs — all that kind of stuff. And maybe the summer'll be interesting enough here so that I'll want to record some of that stuff, too. The page is under heavy construction, but you might want to check it out. At least it gives me something to do.

Once again, we return you to our regularly scheduled program:

After about a week, my parents just decided 'Screw it, the summer's ruined.' There are worse things than Manhattan in June. (What, I don't know. But then, I suppose I've never been to Bombay.) What weirded me out about the whole parental unit thing was how SERIOUS they both were. I really expected something different, to be honest. Like my mom would become hysterical and remain hysterical for a good three weeks. Then Dad would be totally consumed with how hysterical she was, and take like a week off from the Publisher (like anyone is there in the summer anyhow) and be around to comfort her. Then, after about three weeks, my mom would realize that there was INSURANCE money coming for a new house and a lot of NEW decorating. And then she would suddenly get chipper. Dad would immediately flee back to Manhattan — he hates decorating binges — and all would be well with the family's world.

I thought too soon. None of this EVER happened. My mom and dad just got really serious and did a lot of meeting with insurance agents, bankers, lawyers, and Uncle Jim (which was REALLY strange). No hysterics from Mom. No calls to the real estate agent or the decorator. Nothin'. Too weird.

Being a smart aleck is my defense mechanism and can be kind of annoying. (Or so you tell me. Frankly, I think it's endearing.) Needless to say, my suggestions about buying a HOUSEBOAT didn't go over too well. Even Dad wasn't in the mood to take a joke. And then they both kept looking at me in this really CONCERNED way. Now I've been upset about this whole catastrophe. I've cried, but not IN FRONT of people. Yeah. I'm bummed. But we'll come out of it. It's not like anyone DIED or anything. It's not like we're ruined and the insurance company won't pay or something. Life will be screwed up for a while, and then it'll go back to being the way it was. But it's like my mom and dad didn't see it that way. I don't know. Maybe they were more attached to the house than I thought. The house HAS been in my dad's family for a bajillion years.

So, now we're into the whole riding accident thing and my mother not being able to deal with me anymore, but my carpal tunnel is acting up so I'm going to sign off. Check out sarahspage. I think it's kinda cool ;-)

Bye,

sarah@sarahspage.com

BRIEF EXCERPT FROM THE WEB SITE:
What is Southampton anyway?

Southampton is a beach community about 2 hours' drive from Manhattan. Actually it's 2 hours when you leave at 2 in the morning. Any other time there will be so much traffic on the LIE (that's the Long Island Expressway, also known as the largest parking lot in the world) it really takes like FOUR hours. And don't even TRY to get there if you leave Manhattan on a Friday afternoon in the summer unless you have a helicopter.

So why is everyone in the WORLD (that is, the New York world) trying to get to Southampton? Because it is THE place in the summer. Actually, the whole HAMPTON thing is pretty much THE PLACE. That includes Westhampton, East Hampton, Bridgehampton, and Hampton Bays (You really have to stretch it to include Hampton Bays, but then, I'm a snob.). Still, Southampton is THE HAMPTON-est of the HAMPTONS. Totally OLD GUARD. All the houses are HUGE and EXPENSIVE, especially the ones that are right on the water. They are usually surrounded by tall (I mean 10-feet tall) privet hedges, and there are a lot of big estates with private drives so you can't see anybody's house from the road. We lived on a big estate, but I'll get to that later.

So then there's the whole New-York-Country-House-Thing. New Yorkers mostly live in apartments. Sometimes the apartments are pretty nice, but a lot of people have a country house, too. Country houses, I guess, can be anywhere, but people usually have them in

Westchester County, Connecticut, New Jersey, and Long Island. The north shore of Long Island, Connecticut, and Westchester are really nice if you like the country/horse thing. New Jersey and Long Island have real beaches on the ocean. (You mostly summer in New Jersey because you HAVE to, not because you want to; but, as I have said, I'm a snob.)

We were lucky because my grandparents, who are now dead, had a house on an estate in Southampton. It was RIGHT on the water. My grandmother left my father the house because Dad wanted that, and left my Uncle Jim a bunch of money because he wanted THAT. I think we got the better end of the deal. The house had twenty rooms, a guest house, and a quarter mile of private beach front. It was really cool. It had dumbwaiters, and secret doors in the paneling, and an upper garden and a lower garden. And my Mom had JUST finished redecorating. Every year we left in the fall I would go around saying goodbye to the house and hoping it wouldn't be lonely. And every year when we came back, I went from room to room saying hello again.

Please send all comments to webguru@sarahspage.com

📧 To: katie@dundee.net
From: sarah@sarahspage.com
Date: 6-16
Subject: Mitten-Shaped States & Major Head Injuries

Hi Katie,

I'll continue with the story, but first I have to tell you once again how LAME I think this whole weird state is. I've put some facts on the Web site. Did you know that Michigan is shaped like a mitten and that there are more smokers per capita than any state in the nation, save Louisiana? Fascinating. I'm riveted.

NOTHING is the way it should be. You'd think that living in an old farmhouse would be romantic. But this is MICHIGAN, and you'd be WRONG! Living in an old farmhouse is romantic if you do it in suburban Connecticut — when the house has been gutted and redone by an architect, and the best decorator in Greenwich has ordered vintage quilts for every room. In rural Michigan, living in an old farmhouse means drafty walls, bad plumbing, rodents, and an electrical system so ancient you can't turn on the toaster and the hair dryer at the same time. "Remodeling" means putting in dropped tile ceilings, paneling like the Brady Bunch house, and wall-to-wall carpeting. :-o YUK. Of course Amy says she wants to redo everything. Sure. Like THAT will ever get done. She couldn't even pull together a REAL wedding like any NORMAL person.

I mean, like, how do you even KNOW people are married unless they have a REAL wedding? Anyway, I've pretty much decided that this pioneer thing isn't all it's cracked up to be.

Check out the page yet? There's a cool picture of my BIG ACCI-DENT. It's amazing the horse show photographer actually GOT that shot. What I don't get is how he EVER approached my dad. Like, what did he say, "Here's a picture of your daughter's last moments on earth. Five-by-seven or eight-by-ten?"

The really scary thing is that my dad DID buy the picture.

But I'm going out of order. Here's what happened: We went back to Manhattan, and BOY was the apartment depressing. I just had to get out of there, so I decided to hang out at the riding stable in Oyster Bay. I mostly ride on weekends, so they were pretty surprised to see me. But what else was there to do?

The only hitch in my plan was that I've never really liked that hoofed TERRORIST people insist on calling a horse. He's sneaky and runs out at fences and rubs me off under trees and stuff like that. But I'm pretty gutsy, so I figure the one horse show can't kill me, right?

Darn near killed my mother, though. I don't remember any-thing after I entered the ring. But Mom could write a MOVIE SCRIPT about it. It wasn't pretty. He tried to stop at every fence. It was: Dodge to the right. Dodge to the left. JUMP! Dodge to the left. Dodge to the right. JUMP!

The third fence was my Waterloo. He was barreling along, and then, without any warning, came to this screaming dead halt. I was SOOO mad. I cracked him real hard with the whip. He reared back, heaved himself over, caught his feet in the rails and plunged, snout first, into the turf.

Unfortunately, my snout was only a short distance behind.

I woke up in the apartment. The first thing I remember hearing was the distant sound of traffic. And my mother calling "Sarah, baby, can you hear me? It's Mom."

She cried for like an hour when I opened my eyes. Then the doctor started to ask me questions. Like, "What's your name?" (nailed that one), "How old are you?" (no brainer); but then he hit the real toughies like "What month is it? Where do you go to school?" I swear to God, Katie, I had NO idea. Quick thinking on the doctor's part, too, because when he saw my eyes start to glaze over, he asked my mother if she could get some hot towels — like I was giving birth or something. He never used the towels.

Losing your memory is like the weirdest thing that ever happened to you. Alzheimer's patients must feel this way. It's like the here and now is crystal clear. (Except for the Freddy-from-Friday-the-13th-drove-an-icepick-through-my-head headache.) But everything else was really far away. School, the hurricane, the horse — they were just like wiped clean. The only thing left was today and tomorrow. Yesterday just didn't seem to matter. It was totally washed away.

Gradually — after about 4 days — things started to trickle back. Which, to be honest, was mildly depressing. When I couldn't remember, I was free from the stress of losing the house and then how weird Mom and Dad were. I hate change. I like my life to stay the same. It nearly killed me to have to make the switch from the Middle School to the Upper School. And I don't know WHAT I'm going to do about this whole college thing in a couple of years. Guess I have a lot of re-pressing to do. So, anyway, once I was conscious again, I tuned into the fact that the units were downloading this major VIBE.

I HATE being a kid. You feel like you want to know what's going on, but you probably don't REALLY want to know what's going on. And then you have no real control over the whole operation, so it's like, who cares?

While I was groggy everything else felt really far away. I almost DIDN'T care. That must be how people feel when a piece of their life ends — like if you move or someone dies or you get divorced or whatever. There's a part of your life that just fades into the background, even if you loved it a lot. And soon, you can't even remember it really well anymore. That's kinda how it felt having my memory gone. But I didn't let it worry me too bad because, of course, my life hadn't changed THAT much. BTW — on sarahspage I have a list of all the things I could remember and all of the things I couldn't remember. Check it out and let me know what you think.

So, anyway, like I was saying, I started to feel okay again, but my mom was OVER THE EDGE. I know she's not like the most easygoing mom around (Okay. Okay. But it's not like yours is EITHER.) Mom really took my little spill HARD. I heard her telling my father that we needed to sell the horse "sooner than we thought." I really don't get the "sooner than we thought" part. But maybe they found the horse's terrorist union card.

THEN Mom started talking about sending me to live for the summer with my SISTER in MICHIGAN! Yikes! I mean, Amy WANTS to live in Michigan and I'm sure SOME of the other people who live in Michigan want to live there. But I DON'T. I want to live in New York where all my New York friends are, and go to Southampton in the summer where most of my New York friends go, and take the train to the North Shore on weekends to ride my horse. (Hopefully, my next one will be slightly retarded and docile.)

YES! I admit it! I'm a yuppie-in-training. A rich kid! An elitist! A snob! Call me anything you like but don't cut my umbilical cord to Manhattan Island. I agree that New York is the most provincial place on earth. I mean, for crying out loud, NORMAL kids are all waiting to get their drivers' licenses. Not us New York kids. We don't need drivers' licenses. We live in Manhattan. I mean how old was that guy your sister married — like 30 — and he had NEVER had a drivers' license?! I don't think my grandmother ever went outside the 10 square Upper-East-Side blocks surrounding her apartment. (And if she did, she used a map.)

Anycase. We are provincial. Like the ancient Romans. (Wasn't that class cool?) We think we are WAY better than all those weird Visigoths out there. We establish imperial outposts (Greenwich, Locust Valley, Oyster Bay, Summit, Hamptons), we plant a flag, we build our aqueducts and we demand that everyone we colonize accept our culture or we feed them to the lions. (Actually, we New Yorkers just act really snotty and superior, but you get the idea.) Yes. That's me. HAIL MAYOR GIULIANI!

Now my sister Amy, as you know, was way too earthy crunchy for New York. Don't know how my mother (Madam Bergdorf Goodman herself) ever gave birth to such a tree-hugger. But let's just say it's lucky she didn't stop with Amy. Not like they MEANT to have me — there's 10 years between Amy and me. By the way, there's like 7 years between you and Claudia. So, like waddaya think? Ever ask your Mom and Dad about THAT one?

So, all the time I was an adorable, toddling yuppie-to-be in my little applique outfits from Le Petit Bateau, Amy was begging to go to summer camp on a ranch in Colorado. I think the only reason she went to Yale instead of someplace like

University of Arizona is that, once she got in, she thought my parents would both end up in therapy if she didn't enroll. Dad especially. Turns out my grandfather wouldn't let Dad go to Yale because he said it was a Red school. Gramps was stuck in the McCarthy era. Dad would just have DIED if Amy didn't go, and when he told her that story, Amy caved. Dad figured it was because she really DIDN'T want the family to go another generation without tickets to The Game. Actually, Amy liked the idea of Yale as a Commie enclave. THAT'S why she went.

Jeff was at Yale Med at the time — and had just inherited his family's farm. Turns out his mom and his grandparents like all died the same year (major funeral-parlor summer), and left him the family farm. And Amy thinks — "Wow, romantic. I'll go to live in Michigan on a farm with a country doctor." And Dad thinks, "Well, at least he went to Yale." And Mom thinks, "Well, at least he's a doctor." And Sarah thinks, "Well, at least I get to stay in New York."

And Sarah was WRONG. Getting back to the part where I'm lying in my sickbed listening to my parents — Mom says they're going to sell the horse and send me to live with Amy in Michigan. Why? Turns out my mother thought my accident was — get this — A VEILED SUICIDE ATTEMPT. Boy, can I plan 'em, or can I plan 'em? No messy razor blades or pills for me. No splat on the sidewalk from 20 stories up. Nope, I'd rather get all dressed up and take a dive into a brush box. Now THAT's the way to go! Elegant. VERY Christopher Reeve.

So there is no WAY I can persuade her I haven't tried the old equine hasta la vista. And — I hear her talking with my dad — "If Sarah's THIS upset over the house going in the ocean, imagine how she'll feel LATER." Well, I know that house-hunting and decorating sprees with my mother can be tough, but not enough to kill yourself over. Normally, I would expect my dad to come to my defense. But like I already explained, this summer they have NOT been acting predictably. So Dad AGREES with her. And before I know it, I have a plane ticket to Michigan and a reservation at Chez Manure Pile in the Barney Suite!

So, that brings you pretty much up to date with how I GOT here. But I have sooooo much to fill you in on since. It's kind of hard. Jeff is nice, but Amy and I are having just this TEENSY WEENSY bit of trouble finding common ground. She thinks we should do the horse thing together. So check out the page. I was able to do this cool animation of the house going into the ocean. More tomorrow. Going to sleep ',-)

Type at you later,

S

To: katie@dundee.net
From: sarah@sarahspage.com
Date: 6-17
Subject: The Local Scene, Misguided Adventures in Animal
Preservation

Hi K-woman,

You know, I have to admit mornings here are kinda cool.
Michigan is this really WET state. Supposedly they have like 5
gazillion lakes. All around are these boggy marshy places with
cattails and ducks and stuff. In the morning, if the air is just a
little bit cool, all this fog blankets the place and floats down
and settles in the low areas.

Amy and Jeff's house is high up on a hill. The early farmers
didn't have any flies landing on them, boy. They said to them-
selves — "Lotta water round here. Gotta be up high." So all the
old farmhouses are on the highest ground. Lemme tell ya, it
also helps with the mosquitoes who are big enough to MUG
you. From my window, I can see the whole surrounding area.
And in the morning, the mist pools down in this one area of
their property that's marsh, and drapes right along the stream
that runs through. And the spiders build webs overnight and
the mist drops collect on them so they look like these white
pieces of paper scattered all over the fields. Norman Rockwell,
eat your heart out.

So, I do get this small twinge of "this is nice." But then I say to myself, "SNAP OUT OF IT." There isn't a THING to look at for miles other than farm fields and the occasional house. And Amy and Jeff live on a DIRT ROAD. Yes, you heard me. DIRT. You bump and rattle all the way to their house. And then there's all this overgrown grass along either side. So I asked Amy, "Why doesn't the town or the village keep the roads better?"

And Amy says, "Sarah, this isn't Greenwich, Connecticut."

Okay, DUH. What was your first clue? The John Deere cruising down Main Street, or the gas station selling LIVE BAIT?

Amy and Jeff have this BIG old barn. MAN those old German farmers made things to LAST. The foundation is made of these HUGE fieldstones that they dragged out of the fields. Or so Amy says. Personally, I think the same aliens that moved those huge statues on Easter Island had a hand in this construction feat. But I'm keeping my opinions to myself.

Since Amy's a teacher, she's off for the summer. What else do you do with a $100,000 Yale education but go to work in a backwoods school for $26,000 a year? Somebody put this woman in charge of a mutual fund!

Jeff is an okay guy. He's outta here every morning at 7 a.m., dressed in his scrubs. His best feature is the way he cuts through the Donnelly family hysteria. You'd think as hip as Amy is she'd be really laid-back. Nope. We both got it from Mom — just in different ways. I'm like this really high-energy prepster and she's this whirling dervish druid. So Mom must have given Amy the idea that I was totally on the edge because the day I arrived she was all HOVERING over me in a hide-the-knives kind of way. Finally Jeff chimes in with, "Amy, would you knock it off. Your sister's fine. If she OD's, I'm a doctor. Remember?" It cut through the stress, and we all laughed and felt better.

They have adopted this dalmatian dog. Ever since that movie came out, all these people have been buying dalmatians for their kids. Well, if people want something spotted, they should just buy a hyena, because it'd be less wild than a dalmatian. A lot of these spotted maniacs end up in shelters. Amy can't just adopt a greyhound like any respectable bleeding heart. She hears about the dalmatian glut and has to have one of THOSE.

Remember that hockey game we used to play — the one where the puck is carried on those little streams of air. And it just whizzes all over — BOINK, BAM, CRASH. Okay, that's Ellie. She just RUNS all over the place. If she can't stop, she slams into the wall. I guess she's about 3 years old. She chews everything. Last night I walked in, and she was under my desk chewing on my computer cables. Okay, so THAT stopped in a hurry. But then, she looked at me real mad, jumps up on my bed and pees on my pillow WHILE SHE'S LOOKING AT ME. It was a real, take THAT moment. I think the people that owned her were tired of having their stuff destroyed.

Two pairs of docksiders and one Dooney & Bourke purse later (ouch that hurt), I guess she decided I had felt enough of her pain. Two nights ago around midnight, she trotted up the stairs and got into bed with me. And I don't mean she just LAY down at the bottom of the bed. She jumped up, stepped on my head and used her nose to pry open my arms, which I had clenched tight on the covers under my chin (It's kinda chilly here at night in June.). Then she dove under the covers, turned once and lay with her back to me and her head ON THE PILLOW. Gotta respect a woman that knows what she wants. I know you're thinking, "YUK!" But I'm telling you, your standards for YUK change out here. Besides, she's really warm.

So I get up at 7 a.m. Yes ME, up at 7. Believe me, it's not of my own free will. FIRST of all, out here in the sticks, the whole WORLD shuts down at 10 p.m. I'm SERIOUS. Get this through your head, THERE ARE NO GREEK DELIS. You can't just hook up with your friends at 9 o'clock and walk half a block to the deli and stay up till midnight sucking down egg creams, talking about who's dating who. Or decide to go to a movie and walk three blocks to the theater. I don't know WHERE the kids are or WHAT they do. It's impossible to do ANYTHING if you don't drive. Though, I hear that most kids around here drive tractors when they're like 6 years old. Still, all I know is when you look out from my sister's dining room (and I use the term loosely), you can see the lights of like 3 houses. Then at 10, it's dark. It's depressing.

So I stay up another hour or so writing e-mail to you and working on the page. But then Ellie jumps on the bed and barks at me, and I'm usually kinda sleepy anyway.

Why? Because she gets me up at 7! Licks my face until I wake up. Like I said, your standards for YUK change around here. But yesterday, even if I wasn't awakened by the saliva reveille, I would have heard the old fart farmer. Amy and Jeff's nearest neighbor is this 86-year-old farmer. And he was out fertilizing the corn field. Now, I don't know how YOU feel about an 86-year-old man riding on a huge John Deere tractor, but frankly I'm glad I was still in bed. Turns out he also tries to help Amy out by cutting the edges of her yard so she doesn't have to mow. Problem is, he can't see really well. So he took out like 7 of her rose bushes. His name is Door. As in "Close the _____." People have these weird names out here. What ever happened to "Chaz" and "Mitsy"?

By 7:30 the day is in full swing and I'm drinking coffee. Not cappuccino. Not latte or mocha. Regular old coffee. Then I go for a walk. First, the dog needs it. Second, I do. To be honest, I'm finding it hard having so much time to THINK about things. It's not that I mind the thinking so much. It's that I mind the stillness. If I'm going to have to ponder my life, I want my feet moving while I'm doing it. Anyway, the field is pretty neat because all the hay is growing tall. It smells like — well, sweet hay. And as I wade through the tall grass, all these eeny weeny grasshoppers ping away from me in every direction. Like HEY WHAT THE ___! You're walking through my HOUSE!

This morning when I got back, Amy and Jeff were deep in discussion. Jeff was pretty frustrated. He was saying, "Look, Amy, you just can't bring your urban-vegetarian opinions to the country. Those animals don't belong around humans."

"What animals?" I said.

"Jeff says we've got wild cats in the barn."

"Cool," I said.

"Not so cool," Amy said. "He thinks they've got rabies or something."

"Well. Why don't you just get rid of them?" I asked.

It was one of those moments when you know you've taken the side of one married person, and that one looks really smug and the other looks like you've just sold them out. Well, Amy looked like I'd just sold her out.

"You see. Your sister loves animals and even she agrees."

"Wait. What did I agree to?"

"Oh, nothing," says Amy, real calm and cool, just like Mom. "Jeff is going to shoot them."

Okay, so like in a nanosecond Amy and I were standing shoulder to shoulder for the first time in our LIVES. I guess I didn't realize that you couldn't just call up a SERVICE to get rid of wild cats in your barn. Like you do with roaches. You call the service, you leave for the summer and when you come back, they're gone. Obviously they KILL the roaches. But I guess I thought the Cat Removal Service would just RELOCATE them. But, like I discovered, there IS no Cat Removal Service.

"Well," says Jeff, "What do you ladies plan to do?"

Amy looks at me and I look at her. "Relocate them," I said.

"Oh," says Jeff in a real know-it-all tone. "That'll work."

You would not BELIEVE what the day was like, but we did it. I think I have the worst case of poison ivy I have ever had in my life and like a hundred mosquito bites.

First, we went out and got some cat food. We got like 20 cans because we had no idea how it was going to work. It was kinda cool doing this with Amy. It gave us something to talk about.

So we got this big cardboard box. We put an open can of food in the middle of the barn, and hid behind some hay bales. So then, one of the cats comes over and WHAM! I take a flying leap and catch him under the box.

Well, that's how it was SUPPOSED to work. Actually, the first few times the cat zapped away when he saw me coming. After about 5 cans of cat food, I got one. Boy, lemme tell ya. These cats were WILD. That thing started hurling itself against the sides of the box. I sat on it until Amy raced over. Then we slid this other piece of cardboard underneath the box and both held on tight until we could turn it over. I got a couple of scratches, cuz this cat paw kept reaching out of any opening and swiping in the air — like a scene from an alien movie.

So, in a brief 2 hours we had our first cat. Pooh on Jeff, we both thought. We held the box between us, and got it into the back of Amy's truck. (Yes Amy drives a pickup truck. I won't even TELL you about the country music she listens to.) We taped the box shut and motored on over to the local animal rescue place. THAT's when our plans started to fall apart.

We stood there, braced against each other, holding on to the Mexican-jumping-bean box. The woman behind the desk just LOOKS at us. So we tell her about the cats. She tells us that if they took in every wild animal in everybody's backyard, they'd go out of business.

So this was TOTALLY NOT what we'd expected to hear. We both just stood there, stumped.

"Do you have any suggestions about what we should DO with these cats?" Amy finally asked.

The woman shrugged and looked down at her paperwork, "Why don't you just shoot 'em?"

So we're like, "WHAT is it WITH you people!?"

On our way back to Amy's we decided we'd just have to take the cats out to the woods behind Amy's house. They could live there with the other wild animals. (Actually, once they saw this feline spawn coming, the woodland fauna would probably vacate the neighborhood. But still.)

We drove through the fields, lugged the box a few hundred yards into the woods, set it down, quickly ripped the top off and ran. So did the cat. Disappeared into the woods. I have to admit, the cat did look kinda gross — like it was sick. But we're like, "Okay. THIS is a PLAN."

All told, we relocated 12 cats. We ran out of cat food and had to go to the kitchen for tuna fish. But I think it cost less than $50. Not bad.

About 10 p.m. we were sitting up, congratulating ourselves on what a good job we'd done, when Jeff comes in and says, "Well girls, I'd like you to listen to something."

So we all go to the back porch and listen. It was like this chorus, coming from the barn. This "Reow. Reeeoww. REEEEOW!"

"Obviously, they liked the menu," said Jeff. "Good work. Now they know if they stay, you'll feed them."

I went to bed listening to the cat chorus with Ellie growling softly. You know what she was thinking too. "Damn cats. Lemme at 'em." I didn't sleep well, and I was up before Amy and went out to take a walk.

Ellie and I were out for about an hour. I had almost forgotten about the cats, until I reached the edge of the yard. There they were. Hiding in the tall grass. All the wild cats. An alien tribe, with a leader who said, "This, men, is the place of the sacred can-opener. It will be our new homeland. Tonight, when the humans are asleep, we take the house."

It's weird: You have this idea about cats as cuddly, domestic animals. It messes with your mind to see them wild like this. It's as if your favorite teddy bear suddenly grew fangs or something. And I'm like, MAN, is THIS what happens to you out here?

Ellie went after one and it hissed and scratched her nose.

I stepped up onto the porch.

There was something soft under my foot.

Naturally I leaped back like 20 feet. God only knows WHAT they have out here. In New York if you step in something soft, you KNOW what it is. Well this wasn't THAT. It was a cat. A DEAD cat, I might add. Remember I said some of these cats looked sick? Well this sick one had obviously crawled up to the porch. It knew we had food. Maybe it thought we had a complimentary health plan as well.

Well, it was too late for a feline HMO. So I went inside and got a garbage bag. I toed the body into the bag. YUK standards — out the window.

Jeff opened the back door and looked at me. "Sorry, kid. Not like New York, huh?"

We all had kind of a quiet breakfast. "Well," says Amy, "What do you think we should do about the cats?"

Kate, I don't know what came over me. I just hated these things. I hated them for invading my life, and for being so wild and alien. And for not being New York roaches you can just exterminate. And for not STAYING relocated when they had BEEN relocated. In order to continue living with myself, I'll just chalk the whole thing up to the major head injury:

"Shoot 'em," I said.

I knew Amy just couldn't handle it. So Jeff and I went out at dusk. The cats hunt at night and their eyes gleam in the dark. Jeff had the gun. I held the flashlight. The only thing we need to complete the scene was a ring of covered wagons and the distant sound of howling.

It's hard to talk about, Kate. It's TRUE. I WANTED to kill them. Funny thing. If it had been a REAL wild animal, a wolf or something, I would have felt totally different. I would have been like, "Hey! You can't kill that gray wolf! They're EN-

DANGERED, for crying out loud!" But there was something about these cats. They were this weird mixture of two worlds, domestic little house kitties and totally wild animals. THAT was what made me want to kill them.

I don't know, Kate. I don't know if any of this is right, wrong, or like if it doesn't matter. But we killed them. All 12. Tell ya what. Tonight, I really want to be back in my apartment. If I were, know what I'd do? I'd call you up and we'd go to the deli and I'd get about 2 hours of Kate therapy to recover. Then we'd schedule a facial at Georgette Klinger and about 5 hours of shopping. Sound good?

Gotta go. Ellie's barking bedtime.

Your friend, the felinocidal assassin.

S

To: katie@dundee.net
From: sarah@sarahspage.com
Date: 6-18
Subject: Sad

Hi K,

I'm sad tonight. It's one of those strange nights when I just can't figure out why. It's late. Like 11 o'clock, and I just don't feel like sleeping. I ache to be back in New York. I want the brightness of the lights and the commotion and to walk down to the deli and have an egg cream. And to not be alone. It's so dark outside, and so still and quiet. The mist eats up all the sound. All you can hear is the faintest of crickets.

I hate when I'm like this. It's maudlin. I can't even be funny. And I do stupid things like putting my feelings down on paper — uh, you know, on screen. I don't think I can describe the way I feel. Maybe the e-genies will help me out.

It's funny to cry for a stupid thing like a house. Maybe it's feeling so sad and guilty about the cats. I can't believe I'm becoming the kind of person that would actually help shoot a bunch of cats. Is this what happens to you when your life changes? You could become ANYONE, even a person that kills cats? A million people I don't know probably died today. I guess that's something to cry over. But I feel like I've lost a part of my life. Maybe it's my parents. It's not like, you know,

I bought a toy and it broke, and Mom says, "Don't worry honey, we'll buy you a new one." I'm not getting that we'll-buy-you-a-new-one vibe from them. I'm getting this major, IT'S-OVER vibe.

Why does a thing like this happen? It's got to have a reason. I can't believe I'm sitting here on the prairie for no good reason. I mean, I feel so useless. Since I've left New York, I feel like I've left ME. Who IS this person clacking on the keyboard anyway? I mean, is it really true? Am I really just a Manhattan kid, with a horse and a prep-school enrollment? So I lose a house, leave the city, and I'm done? I end up just this cat-killing, Web page, e-maniac zombie? Tonight, Katie, I feel like admitting it: Yes that's all I am. I just MISS everything so much. Why am I so homesick? It's not like I'm twelve at my first summer camp. Maybe it's just the night — tonight, I mean — but I can't shake this feeling that something's really gone.

And what if it is? What'll I do then? I can't live on a Web page. Funny. The real-est thing to me right now is just bytes on a chip. Sometimes I feel like this screen is a window. Like now — like I can reach out and find you. And the site — with everything on it. It's so REAL to me. But, then I think it's just a bunch of stupid electrons.

You know, as I've been driving around with Amy and looking at things around here, I realize how DIFFERENT a life we've lived. I gotta face it. We're rich kids. We SAY we understand that everybody doesn't have a country house or go to private school and stuff like that. But everyone we KNOW does — so I guess it seems like everybody ELSE does. We're so totally into our OWN world we don't see any other.

I guess it ends up making me feel like my New York life is really fragile and maybe not so real after all. Maybe it's just seeing the house going into the ocean. But maybe being out here has made me realize what a petri dish we've lived in. And this big mad scientist in the sky could like, stir things up, and we'd be totally TOAST. And yet I LOVE my life. And I don't know how to be Sarah without it.

I'm sorry to lay all this on you. And you've been so good, filling my mailbox and keeping me happy. I'm sorry. I'm just out of context. WHO I AM just isn't clear like it always has been for me. And I have this really scary feeling that the whole WHO-I-AM thing is kinda like our poor old house. One day it'll be sucked out with the tide.

Think if I go kill some innocent animal I'll feel better? Chipmunk this time? Field mouse? Bunny rabbit?

Ellie just groaned from the bed. It's her will-you-get-over-yourself groan. Soon to be followed by the get-your-butt-over-here-and-warm-up-this-bed barking serenade. Nothing like a demanding dalmatian to keep me from doing any profound soul-searching.

Thanks for listening.

Sad Sarah   ',-(

📧 To: katie@dundee.net
From: sarah@sarahspage.com
Date: 6-21
Subject: Horse!

K-meister,

You're right. I should stop worrying so much. If I can't figure out what's wrong with M&D, I should just ASK them. It's probably nothing at all. And what if it's the worst it could possibly be? Heck, I've dealt with seeing my home go in the ocean; I guess I can deal with a lot of other stuff too. And my old life isn't totally gone. It's just gone for the summer. And, I mean, how long can one summer possibly be? I'll do some new things, meet some new people, become a little enlightened, and then go back to New York and keep on being a yuppie in training. And I'll probably get an A on my what-I-did-for-my-summer essay. No problem.

Amy is on your same cheer-Sarah-up wavelength. When I came downstairs she was on the phone with Mom. Mom and Amy have been talking a lot lately. I guess it's cuz I'm here. Anyway, Amy was saying, "No, Mom. It won't cost anything," (which I thought was a weird thing for her to say), "It's my friend Dave. And we can keep it here. Okay, Sarah's here. I have to tell her."

"Tell me what?"

"How'd you like another horse?"

Wow. Hit me like a ton of bricks. This just overwhelming YES bubbled up inside me. I don't know why. It just felt like this familiar thing from my REAL life. Horse, yes. NOW we're talking.

"Okay, Sarah. I think I have to tell you we're not talking about a fat, shiny show horse that you can just get on and ride."

I was stupid. I was like NOT even listening. All I could think of was, horse, yes, horse, yes, horse, yes.

"Whatever, Amy. What's the plan?"

So then she told me. She has this friend Dave who keeps horses — thoroughbreds. This is Quarter Horse-Appaloosa country out here, so I was kinda surprised. Anyway, he rescues track horses. You know, Belmont Park can look pretty seedy if you walk around some of the barns. I can't IMAGINE what some of these second and third rate tracks in Ohio are like. So Dave goes around Michigan and Ohio, finding horses that are going to be sold for meat because they have some problem. Then he takes them, rehabilitates them, retrains them, and even gives them new names. Some become show horses. The really bad cases he retires out to pasture, or finds someone who maybe only wants to trail ride or maybe just keep the horse and pet it. So, anyway, he calls Amy, cuz they're friends and he knows I'm here for the summer and says, "I think I have a horse for your sister." He thinks this horse has a future.

So here's the deal on this horse: Dave was at the track when the ACCIDENT happened. Whenever Dave goes scouting for horses he has his vet friend with him. These horses just pound around the track. I never thought of it before, but they always go counterclockwise. So their left front leg takes a real beating. This horse went DOWN in a pile. Which is what happens when they break a leg. So everyone goes running onto the track. And the owner is saying "Shoot him" — or "Inject him" — or whatever. And Dave's vet friend is saying "Wait." So having the horse put down, then hauled away, is going to cost the owner money and he says to Dave and the vet friend, "You want 'im you got 'im." So they put this ice boot on the horse, shoot him up full of dope and haul him home.

Turns out the vet guy didn't think this was a TOTALLY broken leg. He says to Dave, who says to Amy, that a lot of times a small bone in their ankle chips off. If they can immobilize the leg and bring the swelling down, they can go in and remove the bone chip and *voilà,* good as new. And since this Dave-friend-guy is a vet, he can do the bone chip removal thing. No problem.

So Dave doesn't have time for ANOTHER horse and wants to know if Amy's sister is interested in this one. And will we come over and look at this de-chipped horse?

So, like I said: horse, horse, horse, horse. Let's GO!

Love,

horsecrazy sarah   < __ ~

✉ To: katie@dundee.net
From: sarah@sarahspage.com
Date: 6-22
Subject: Dim Yuppies & Equine Studies 101

Hi ya K,

Whatta day! Amy and I spent the morning going over her barn setup. Lucky thing that before Jeff's relatives all up and died, this was a working farm. They had cows, but from like ancient times there were still a couple of stalls left over. And there're lights and running water. So we're like, COOL.

But here's the real whacked-out thing. I've been around horses since I was four. You know the way my parents are — they've always wanted this English manor lifestyle. Of course neither of them ever went NEAR a horse, but their precious daughters were all dolled up in tiny little jodhpurs and itsy bitsy little hunt coats at preschool age. Amy never really got into the whole horse-show-scene thing — though she's a good rider. She was always more into the trail-riding-pleasure deal. So both of us have been around horses and taking lessons for like FOREVER and neither of us know the FIRST THING about them! Where WE rode, you get there and the groom brings your horse out all ready to ride, then you ride and then you get off and give it back to the groom. You never really see what goes on behind stage. Who knew there was SO MUCH?

We're trying to put this barn together to get ready for this horse, so we go to the feed store to buy some horse food. And this guy asks us what kind of feed we want to get. We like, look at each other. So I reach real deep into my memory bank and say, "Oats." Amy looks at me real proud like, "Good answer!" Only the guy didn't think so. Turns out there's like all these different KINDS of oats. There's this thing called sweet feed, then feed with more corn in it, and pellet feed, and all these special mixtures. When he got through with us, the guy must have thought we were the dimmest pair of yuppies he'd ever come across. He DID eventually get the idea that we needed some guidance, because he started saying things like, "and I'm sure you'll want wormers, and fly spray and bedding." There's like a million different kinds of all that stuff too. I'm so SURE he gave us 10 or 15 different things we really DIDN'T need just to run up Amy's bill. Problem is, since we didn't know what we needed in the first place, there was like NO WAY to find out the stupid-yuppies-will-buy-this stuff.

We hauled all the stuff back home in Amy's truck. And then we go over to Dave's to see the horse.

Thing is, Amy never really PREPARED me to meet her friend Dave. I knew something was out of the ordinary when we drove down this dirt road (It's like a big thing to find a paved road out here.), tall grass growing on either side, and pulled into Dave's driveway. There were these rows of neatly planted marigolds all the way up the driveway and this impeccably trimmed lawn. Outside the barn, these elaborate wooden flower boxes have flowers pouring out of them. There's this tidy brick walk leading from the barn to the house — with roses growing along it. So I say to Amy, "Dave's wife keeps a nice garden." And Amy says, "No — Dave's friend, Matt, really likes gardening." Then out of the house pops Dave with his friend Matt — the vet guy.

I gotta tell you, these guys seemed so out of place out here in the middle of NO-where. I'm thinking, do you guys KNOW this is Michigan? Did you just try to head to the 'burbs from Greenwich Village and take a wrong turn somewhere, or what? And of course, Amy has found them.

Both guys are tall, thin, good-looking, short hair, in designer jeans and cowboy boots. Dave comes up to Amy takes her hand, and says, "Hey, Babe. SOOOO glad you came." Then kiss-kiss on the cheek. Amy says, "Hi, Matt," and Matt just kind of nods. Dave: "And this is The Sister..." Well, I don't know how I feel about being The Sister, but Dave seems to have this way of just befriending everyone. Still holding Amy's hand, he puts his arm around my shoulder and says,

"Let's go see the patient."

Dave's barn is IMMACULATE. It looks as if he dusts with Pledge. By the time we stroll down the aisle, Matt is already outside the horse's stall. He's rolling gauze and stuff and putting it in this canvas bag. There's a note pinned to the bag that says, "Things for Sarah's horse."

SARAH'S horse.

Inside the stall the light is really dim and I can't see what I'm looking at. Dave says, "In you go, girl." So in I go.

K — I have NEVER seen such a thin horse. Really, he was a skeleton draped in horsehide. His left front leg was wrapped to the knee in gauze and stuff. His head hung low. I scratch behind his ear. He nickers.

Love. I'm in LOVE.

"What's his name?"

"Grand Traverse Bay."

"Catchy."

"Your sister told me you were a wiseass."

"No, really. Why'd you pick that name?"

"Oh, that's a wonderful story. I always try to name horses after something that has a pleasant memory for me. I feel like it gives them a fresh start. Matt and I took a trip once to this beautiful place in northern Michigan on Grand Traverse Bay. La voilà."

Well, I guess it's good that the two of them aren't real fond of taking trips to, say YPSILANTI.

And I'm thinking how do these guys survive with all these armed hillbillies around?

He says, "Sar, can I ask you a question?" You know that people are determined to be on familiar footing with you when they start shortening your name to "Sar."

"Yeah, what?"

"Would you be offended if I asked to see you ride?"

"I don't care." Which was true.

So I got up on Dave's horse — this BEAUTIFUL thoroughbred which he swears looked JUST AS THIN as Traverse Bay when he came in (liar, liar, pants on fire). I rode around a little bit while Dave says things like, "Oh, hun, that's beautiful. Shorten your reins, hun," and stuff like that. Funny, I thought my first ride after the accident would be scarier — but it wasn't, with Dave there and on this rock-solid horse. And, at least he had the good sense not to ask me to jump anything because I think I would have had to throw up.

"Well, I must say," he says, "you ride with panache."

Ah, yes. At last the recognition I deserve. But then he says, "Let's go through the barn and see how much you know about stable management."

You know those dreams you have when you are sitting at your desk waiting to take the SAT, and the teacher hands you the test and it's written in Japanese and you wake up screaming? Yeah, well we've already talked about the feed store embarrassment. I'll spare you the details and just say that I failed barn management.

Amy wasn't much help. She kinda stood back picking at her cuticles. Mom hates that. So Dave is kinda looking back and forth at both of us.

"Well, girlfriends, you've got a lot to learn. We know one thing, in about 2 years, when this horse is all polished and retrained, you sure will be able to ride him. Question is, can you get from here to there in one piece?"

Ouch. That hurt.

"Um. I think we can." I said. Whatta LAME thing to say. This must be what it feels like in a job interview that's going really bad.

Dave lit a cigarette. Marlboro Lights. He blows this long, elegant puff of smoke and leans back against the fence.

"Well I guess you can't kill him. Let's just focus on getting you through the next few weeks."

So then he takes us back to the stall and tells us all this STUFF. You think the feed store was bad. I had no idea how much stuff there is to do to one broken-legged horse. There's the bute (it's some kind of pain killer) he has to take twice a day, and the bandages and then all the stuff that has to go on the wound and the tape and the how-do-you-get-him-around and the what-do-you-look-for. On and on and on. Dave showed me how to bandage the leg — we practiced on Traverse's other leg. And the whole time he's making it really clear that the only way to learn is to do it MYSELF, and he is NOT going to be running over to chez Amy every day because we can't find the roll of tape.

So I suppose you've guessed by now that I'm wondering what I've gotten myself into. It's really weird. I felt so competent up there riding with Dave's fabulous athletic horse under me. But kneeling down there in the shavings, futzing with a roll of tape, I felt just like a doofus. Funny, too, because I guess most people would think that the riding part is harder. But when you have everything — nice horse, good coach — it really isn't. I suppose it's kind of like the life we've lived. Good parents. Good schools. Why should life be hard? (With the possible exception of Trigonometry.) It's not like we grew up in the projects and had to dodge gang members on our way to class. I guess I've really had everything — except some solid experience in shoveling manure.

I still don't know how we got that horse on the trailer. I guess I never really understood what people meant when they'd call a horse "three-legged lame." Now I do. That horse was literally like — one, two, three HOP; one, two, three HOP. Dave drove REALLY CAREFULLY over to our place and we got him in his stall and bedded him down for the night.

Before I started this e-mail, I spent some time working on the page. I thought I'd better record the whole regimen of what I have to do to this horse and like all the barn management stuff. It's kinda interesting and writing it all down makes it so

I won't forget. Besides, you can see how we've got the barn all set up.

Type at you later.

sarah@sarahspage.com

To: katie@dundee.net
From: sarah@sarahspage.com
Date: 6-22
Subject: Old Myths Debunked

Hi K-girl,

I know I'm weird sending two e-mails back-to-back, but I couldn't sleep. I had to go out to the barn and check on Traverse. Ellie just looked at me. She was already half snoozing in the bed and was totally disgusted that I wanted to go outside. But she followed me anyway. She follows me EVERYWHERE. (See the site for some cool info on dalmatians and their weird quirks.)

He was still alive. Thing was, I just wanted to BE with him. For a few minutes I just stood there looking at him. He was slowly munching his hay. I'm thinking MANGIA, MANGIA. He's just so THIN. Finally, I got up enough courage to go in the stall. I petted him a little bit, and then I just sat down in a corner in the shavings. It was really nice — this clean woody smell and the musty horsey smell from Traverse. I never got to do this before.

Traverse was perfectly fine with my being there. Ellie wasn't too keen on it though. She barked at me a couple of times, but when I didn't listen to her she just shimmied under the stall door and lay down next to me with a disgusted moan.

It was SOOO peaceful. The summer moon glowing through the barn windows was big and orange. And Traverse was eating in this munch, munch, munch rhythm. You won't believe it but I actually FELL ASLEEP.

Then, when I woke up — maybe an hour later, I looked over and it was the most AMAZING thing. Traverse was LYING DOWN with us. Now, I've been told like everyone else that horses sleep standing up. And of course I've never SEEN a horse at night — so like who would know? Well it turns out — and I'm here to verify it — horses sleep lying down. I was so excited to discover it, I was like — get me Geraldo Rivera! I can testify! HORSES SLEEP LYING DOWN.

So then Ellie looks at me in this really sarcastic way she has. She gets up, shakes off the shavings like, "So ARE we going IN now that you've discovered the secrets of the universe?" And since I'd had enough earth-shaking discoveries for one night, I decided she was right and we left Traverse just snoozing there.

Ellie is sitting up in bed looking at me like she's going to start chewing on my computer cables again.

Mañana.

S

To: katie@dundee.net
From: sarah@sarahspage.com
Date: 6-23
Subject: Michigan Basements & My Horse World

K—

Ellie has developed a foolproof way of getting me up in the morning. She hops out of bed and barks twice. Then if I don't get up, she starts pillaging. Usually she begins in my laundry pile. She grabs a sock and throws it up in the air, catches it, shakes it back and forth and then begins ripping it up. She really drags out the tearing part for the best sound effects. She'll yank a bit — *rrrrip* — look at me for a reaction; yank a bit more — *RRRIP* — look at me again. Then if I don't react, she lets loose — *RRRRRIP, rip, rip, rip, RRRRRIP*. By that time, I'm out of bed yelling and chasing her around.

I must say though, lately we don't usually get to that point. She has me pretty well trained to be up by the first two barks.

Nevertheless, the barking over the laundry pile reminded me of one major thing: Before I go horse around, I have to do laundry. Laundry may sound like a mundane task to you. You, however, live in an apartment with a lovely little laundry nook. I, on the other hand, am living on the prairie. So let me tell you about MY laundry experience — in other words, my first trip to Amy's basement.

There is this thing called a "Michigan Basement." When you say you live in an old farmhouse, people will invariably ask, "Do you have a Michigan Basement?" I have heard people in the grocery store (such as it is) ask my sister this question. And I'm thinking she's gonna say, "No, actually, our basement is in West Palm. It makes vacationing such a snap."

Turns out people mean something entirely DIFFERENT when they say "Michigan Basement." And it also turns out my sister DOES have one. The short story is that a Michigan Basement means a basement with a dirt floor. But to say that is so bland, so flat. It leaves out so many of the nuances that make a Michigan Basement truly a thing to be remembered. Things like: a rickety staircase that descends at a 45-degree angle where there are no backboards, so you look down into a black abyss; where the last step is missing so you crash, with your laundry falling everywhere, onto the damp, moldy floor. Then there are the cobwebs hanging down like drapes in a Martha Stewart nightmare; and the old wooden barrels left over from kraut-making days; the musty furniture, preserve jars, and the long chest that looks disturbingly like a coffin. Then there are the mice that regard you, unconcerned like, "Howdy, Stranger. You part of the posse that shot the cats? Much Obliged." And then of course there is the heart-thumping anxiety as the one dim, dusty, 75-watt bulb tries valiantly but utterly fails to reach into the basement's murky corners. And you think, WHAT IS OVER THERE!!!??? $^{o}_{o}$-0

Ellie took one sniff down the stairs and looked at me like, "Nope, staying up here, thanks." Then she saw a mouse and came leaping down four steps at a time. She barreled over the coffin, tunneled through all the kraut barrels and came up with the little bugger squealing and clenched tight in her teeth. ATTA GIRL!

Station Break: It's amazing how much I find myself participating in the primal man-against-nature bloodlust.

Back to our program:

So I found the washer, threw in my dirt-covered clothes and made to hightail it out of the basement, when, in a dim corner, something caught my eye. There were all these bottles — jugs, really — lined up together. About 2 dozen of them — and they were all alike. I edged over and uncorked one: the unmistakable smell of alcohol.

Upstairs, Amy and Jeff are having breakfast.

"Hey. You know you have moonshine in your basement?"

"We do?" says Amy.

"Here, take a whiff." I pushed the jug under her nose.

"Oh," says Jeff, "That's homemade wine. My uncle used to make it and my grandfather let him store it in the basement."

Okay. Call me a snob (once again), an elitist, etc. But I NEVER thought I would live in a house that had a bunch of moonshine in the basement. I suddenly felt like I'd washed up onto an episode of the Dukes of Hazzard. I said as much to Amy and Jeff.

"Actually," Jeff says, "that's not moonshine. It's just homemade wine. Moonshine is made out of corn."

How gauche of me. Terribly sorry. I will attempt to avoid such faux pas in the future.

Time to visit the horse.

Maybe it was my early morning Dante-esque wanderings. Maybe it was my late-night snuggle in the shavings, but on my way out to the barn I decided: This is going to be MY world. Mine and the horse. I'm going to do it up like I want it. My horse. My barn. My world.

Traverse had a major case of bed-head. He was standing in his stall with shavings all stuck in his mane and dusted across his back. I slipped the halter over his head and brought him out into the aisleway. Know what? He wasn't limping like the day before. He wasn't NOT limping, but he actually let the bad leg touch the ground and put a little bit of pressure on it. So I'm thinking: Call me Dr. Quinn, Medicine Woman.

Dave was REALLY CLEAR that we had to take things SLOWLY. Traverse could only take A STEP OR TWO, but otherwise was to be confined to his stall. So I counted the steps to get him on the cross ties — it was four, but like, what choice did I have? So I got him on the cross ties and gave him a quick brush down. I scratched along his mane and around his ears and he tilted his head and leaned into me. Cool.

Then I took a deep breath. I had to deal with THE LEG.

Dave had told me that this would be the easiest part of my job. Race horses have had people fussing with their legs all their lives and they usually stand there just really quiet. Turns out he was right. Traverse was fine, but I was my own WORST NIGHTMARE.

I slowly and gingerly unrolled the outer bandage. You're supposed to reroll in the opposite direction as you unroll, to keep things neat, but of course I forgot. Underneath was a large swath of cotton, so I unfolded that. Then underneath THAT were these large gauze pads covering the WOUNDS. Another deep breath. I slowly lifted them away.

So WOW. Dave's friend Matt must be some vet. It was just unbelievable to look at this long, thoroughbred horse-leg and those zipper-rows of stitches. On the outside of his leg, for about 6 or 8 inches, there was one long zipper. Then down the back of his leg, from about 4 inches above his ankle to about 2 inches below it, was another huge incision. I guess they just laid his lower leg open to get a look around and make sure they got that broken piece out of there. And the stitches were just so neat and orderly and in such a perfect line. I'm thinking: Matt, you are a stud.

And then I'm thinking, Traverse, you are a stud too. (Not literally, of course, Traverse is a gelding, but still.) Matt had said that with a surgery like this, a lot depends on the horse. Horses are really freak-a-zoid animals. They really are. Their main trait is nervousness. So like a lot of horses would wake up, take one look at all the stuff wrapped around their leg, take one second to feel the pain and go BLAAAHHHHHH — and totally whack out. But Matt said he had this feeling that Traverse WANTED to get better, that he trusted the guys working on him, and that he would be really levelheaded about the whole thing.

Looking at that leg, I wouldn't have blamed Traverse if he did freak out. Tell you what, if MY leg looked like that, I would be going BLLAAAAAHHHHH! I really would. But Traverse just looked at me like, "Hey, man, I get it. I'm laid up. On the bench. Out for the season. In rehab. Just give me some drugs and some physical therapy, and I'm hanging loose."

Perfect.

So now the problem was getting all that stuff back ON his leg. I tried hard to remember how Dave and I had done it. Okay, first I had to spray this antiseptic on his leg. Now, I don't know how much you know about horses and large aerosol cans. Let's just say that a little spritz of fly spray is enough to send a lot of horses into orbit. So I'm thinking, I'm down here on my knees staring at his leg and he's going to freak out. That's when all of a sudden this FEAR thing came out.

Honest to God, my legs started to shake and my hands started to tremble and all I could think was I didn't want to get kicked in the head. Just not the head thing again. I mean really, how much abuse can your head take? Just look at Muhammad Ali if you don't get what I'm saying.

So I took a second and stepped back. Traverse looked at me. I'm thinking, just give me a minute, horse. I'm having a nervous breakdown here. But then I though about Dave saying he wasn't going to rush over for every little piddling problem. Now, don't get me wrong. This wasn't a piddling problem. It was a really SERIOUS BREAKDOWN. But still. No one was there to help the horse but me, so I had to get a grip.

Tell you what I did. I went over to my trunk and got my helmet and put it on my head. Not doing anything around this horse without my helmet. Traverse saw me put it on and looked at me like, "Don't know if you've noticed, babe, but I'm not really UP for a ride right now."

With the helmet on I felt much better, and sprayed that stuff on his leg. It's like fluorescent yellow so you can see where you've put it, which is cool. Then I gently pressed the big gauze pads back on his leg and took another large blanket of cotton and folded it around.

So then, here was the next problem: I don't have three hands. I had to hold all the cotton and gauze in place WHILE I wound the outer elastic bandage on. I mean, PLEASE! I still don't know how I did it, but let me tell you it wasn't pretty and it wasn't at ALL like Dave did it. All I can say is that it involved taking my boot off to free my big toe and sitting with my foot in the air and my toe pressed to the cotton so that I could wind the bandage. And Ellie is sitting there with the sarcastic look: "Nice technique."

So that took like WAY longer than it was supposed to, but who cares. I did it. I mucked out his stall (who knew a bucket of manure could be so heavy?), refilled his water bucket, and put down some new bedding and some hay. Then I tried to lead him back into his stall.

Well Traverse must have been feeling better because he didn't want to go. He was like "Man, lady, I was in there all night. Can't I do something ELSE?"

Well, I felt bad for him, so I thought for a second. I decided to lead him down the aisle and back. We took it really slowly and he really seemed to enjoy it. He was all sniffing everything, poking his nose everywhere. He even picked some string up in his teeth and flipped it around, like, "Hey, this is cool." Then when I led him back into his stall he was ready to go. I was glad I did that.

So then the rest of the day was Sarah's Barn-World day. I am exhausted and it was so fun. The Web site shows you what I did, but I'll tell you anyway.

First thing was to get the tack room all set. Now I don't know how much you know about tack rooms — but let's just say for horse people they are like your private clubhouse world. Amy and Jeff's barn, being like an old working farm and not a horse stable, wasn't set up with a tack room. But on the opposite wall from Traverse's stall, there was another small stall. So I decided that would be my tack room.

Jeff had helped by bringing out the big box of my horse stuff that my mom had sent. I also bummed a power screwdriver from him and some other doodads. All I can say is: don't mess with a woman who has power tools. By noon I had a saddle rack up — I used part of an old pole and hung it by a hook — a bridle rack, a whole mess of hooks and stuff to hang halters and crops. I hung an old shower rod by some chain to hold my blankets. I even conned Jeff into helping me haul the coffin out of the basement. Tell you what — that coffin made an EXCELLENT tack box — for all Traverse's bandages, gauze, spray stuff, etc. I even put up a shelf on one wall for my helmet and pictures.

I threw a hay bale down in one corner, tossed a blanket over it and put some ratty old pillows against the wall. Voilà! An armchair. I sat down to try it. At that point Ellie — who had been lying on the dirt floor and hating it — jumped up on the new chair. Unfortunately, there wasn't room for her butt and mine because the edges of the hay bale kind of drop off so you have to sit right in the middle. She looked at me like — "MOVE your BUTT."

Okay — so now we have TWO hay bales covered with the blanket and more pillows. Got to keep Ellie happy. She has the power to make my life miserable.

So that was like the infrastructure. The MOST fun part was the accoutrements. How I did all of this is on the Web site, but anyway: I put up a bulletin board for notes and stuff, but mostly for pictures of Traverse. I have this Polaroid camera and I'm going to track his progress. I also have a journal to keep track of what he's like every day. Dave recommended this because if there's a problem I can refer to it when I'm talking to the vet. I had this cool idea and attached little baby food jars to the underside of the shelf by putting Velcro on their tops. I keep little things in them like elastic for Traverse's mane and paper clips and thumbtacks.

Then of course there is the radio — it has its own little corner shelf nailed up. I also made this little fold-down shelf right by the hay bales for my laptop. Jeff actually helped me with it. It's on its own hinge with this metal arm to brace it in place. It's just at the right height for the hay bale. Then, when I'm done, I swing the arm down and the desk lies flat against the wall. Really cool.

Then, of course, I put up pictures all over the walls, and things I ripped from horse magazines, and a big horse-anatomy poster. Tell you what — I am SET. Check out the site! You'll see my tack room.

I hate to be so petty, but there was one teensy thing that bugged me. I kinda expected the box of horse stuff my mom sent from home to contain a SURPRISE. Like all my OLD equipment would be in there, but there would also be a new bridle, or a really pretty new brushes box with a brass nameplate that said "Traverse." It would be SO like my mom to do that. And like she's GOT to know that in the middle of downtown Reed Lake there are no Horse-and-Hound tack shops for me to browse. It would have been nice, but I guess the units are still going through their own weirdness, and I can't expect the usual.

Type at you later,

S

To: katie@dundee.net
From: sarah@sarahspage.com
Date: 6-26
Subject: Amy's Weirdness & Parental Stress Rearing Its
         Ugly Head

K—

Thanks for the pics of you and me. I downloaded them this
morning, and I'm going to put them up on the site and on the
bulletin board in the tack room.

You know, for the last few days I've been so wrapped up in
the horse I forgot to worry about the rental units. But when I
came in tonight from feeding (I walked him down the aisle
again — don't tell anyone), there was Amy on the phone with
Mom AGAIN. I never knew they were so close, but I gotta tell
ya, they're on the phone like all the time now. Never when
I'm around, which gives me the weird feeling they're talking
about ME. That in itself is really weird because if Mom is
spazzing out about me she usually tells me. NOT that I want
to deal with THAT. I'd rather have Amy on the phone with
Mom if she's in her hysterical mood, but still.

So I come through the back door and I hear the end of the
conversation. Amy is saying in this really muffled voice "I'll
talk to her" or "I'll feel her out" or something like that.

So I'm like, "Talk to me about what?"

Amy looks at me like she wasn't prepared for me to be there. She takes this deep breath and says, "Sarah, what do you think about Michigan?"

I sure didn't expect THAT question. So I said the first thing that came to my mind.

"Well, it's not New York."

Amy sighed. "I KNOW it's not New York. But that doesn't answer my question."

She had me there, so I had to think. What DID I think about Michigan? I mean, I guess I had never really thought about anything other than IT'S NOT NEW YORK. And, Amy has been a real sport lately. I really didn't want to hurt her feelings.

"I really like the horse thing Amy. I mean, where else could I just walk out into the backyard and have a horse? It's really great."

She seemed happy I said that. But she still wasn't going to let it lie. "Anything else?"

"Jeez Amy. I want to be nice, I really do. I mean, I said I liked the horse."

She kind of nodded with her hands folded in that totally I'm-open-to-whatever-you-have-to-say liberal attitude thing. "Mmm-hmm."

Well, if she's asking..."I guess we're just different people. I don't know, Amy, we always have been. It's just not New York. It's so REMOTE, and the people all seem so strange."

"You haven't MET any of the people."

"Well they seem strange anyway. It's so quiet, and there's nothing going on, and they don't have Greek delis, and all my friends are in New York, and there aren't any nice shops, and half the roads aren't paved, and I feel so out of place. I don't mean to put your home down, I really don't."

"I asked."

"You DID ask. I think that somebody must WANT to live in Michigan. I just can't imagine that person would ever be ME. I mean, I'm having fun here, and you guys were really good to take me in when Mom couldn't deal with me anymore, but if you're asking what I think, that's what I think. It doesn't TOTALLY stink, but..."

"But it ALMOST totally stinks."

"Without the horse?"

"Without the horse."

"Then, yes. It pretty much would totally stink without the horse."

So now here is the WEIRDEST part. All of our lives Amy and I have had this fundamental lifestyle-clash-thing going on. My mother says it's like the City Mouse and the Country Mouse. They're both little mice, but one is all white and prissy, and the other is this rough-and-tumble field mouse. Charming thought. Frankly I think we're a little more like Israel and the PLO: we deny each other's right to exist. Which is why, once I said what I did, I expected the usual: Amy tosses her head, looks at me with daggers in her eyes and stalks from the room, then won't talk to me for days. This is because it's against her political beliefs to let off steam by yelling and getting all angry like a NORMAL person. It's more PC to just torture someone by not speaking to them. Only fascists yell.

I, of course, usually play my part by running after her and shouting that she thinks she's so open-minded but she really isn't because she's not open-minded toward ME, until she gets to the nearest room and shuts the door in my face. Mind you, she doesn't SLAM the door, because that would be right-wing too. She just firmly, but quietly, SHUTS the door. AARRGH! I HATE THAT. She looks all composed and I look like a raving idiot.

So, I'm all revved up for the conversation to take this turn, but it DOESN'T. Amy presses her hands on the dining room table (such as it is), and sighs.

"I know how you feel being out of place, Sar. That's how I felt in New York pretty much all my life. I mean ME at prep school — come on! Can you believe I ever walked around in those little kilts? Played field hockey? Had a coming-out party? Went to the youth dances at the Meadow Club?" As Amy said this she gestured down to what she was wearing: a pair of Wranglers and one of Jeff's T-shirts that said "Chevy Trucks."

I laughed like I couldn't stop. It was a hoot. Poor Amy! Whatta life!

Then, she looked at me really sad. "I know it's hard being out of place. And I know it really stinks not to live the life you feel like you were born to live. I'm really lucky because I'm really happy here."

Know what? She was right. She WAS really happy. You could SEE it. It's like she finally found a home. I was happy for her and I said so.

"Thanks Sar. I know it's tough on you."

"Aw — c'mon. I'm not THAT fragile. It's only for the summer. It's not like Manhattan Island has been bombed off the face of the earth. I really like being here for the summer and seeing you and the horse IS really great. Don't feel bad for me."

Amy smiled and rubbed my back. "'Kay. I won't."

So I came up here to my room thinking, "Wow. That went well. Amy and I had like a real TALK," when all of a sudden I realized — what about MOM? I mean what did our talk have to do with Mom? And what were they talking about on the phone? And why did that get Amy to ask me what I felt about Michigan? What the HELL? WHAT IS GOING ON HERE!?

I have been thinking and thinking and thinking and I just can't make sense of it. One minute Amy's on the phone with Mom and saying, "I'll talk to her," and the next minute she's asking me what I think about Michigan.

Okay, Kate — you're an outsider. Help! What do you think? What does it all mean? >:-|

Freaking Out,

Sarah

To: katie@dundee.net
From: sarah@sarahspage.com
Date: 6-27
Subject: Right Again

K-meister,

Thanks for the pep talk. You're probably right. Mom probably IS worried that, with the horse and all, I will like it too much and want to stay. Whew! I feel better.

More later.

S

✉ To: katie@dundee.net
From: sarah@sarahspage.com
Date: 6-28
Subject: Sarah's Equine Misadventures Part MCXVV (Is that
        a real number? You're the one who took Latin.)

Kate-ster,

I had SUCH a horrible day! After I e-mailed you this morning,
I went out to see Traverse. He had his back to me in his stall.
And when I said, "Hey T," he turned to me and LIMPED over
to the door. It was probably only two steps, but I could tell he
was limping REALLY BAD.

It was like my heart stopped beating. He looked at me with
his big round eyes like, "It HURTS." So I quickly got his halter
on, tied him up and unwrapped his leg. It was puffed up like
a balloon.

I didn't know what to do. I thought, "What have I DONE to
this poor horse?" I bandaged him up again, gave him some
bute and ran to the house to talk to Amy. Even Ellie had her
tail between her legs.

Amy immediately picked up the phone to call Dave. I tried to
stop her. I told her he would be mad that I had hurt the horse,
and we weren't supposed to be dragging him over here.

"Sarah," she said, "What are you thinking? You just want to bury this and pretend that the horse isn't hurt because Dave will be mad?"

"I mean, I..."

"Sometimes you can be just like Mom," she said, and dialed the phone. I don't know what she meant by that.

In ten minutes, Dave was there with Matt. Matt unwrapped the leg, saw the swelling and looked up at Dave with this LOOK. Dave turned to me.

"You haven't kept him in his stall, have you?"

"I..."

"How far did you take him?"

"Just down the aisle a couple of days. He was so bored and he didn't want to go back to his stall. He was being so good and coming along. Everything seemed fine..."

Then I did something I almost never do. I started to cry right there in front of people. And — except for Amy — people I hardly even KNOW. I just couldn't help it. I had let them all down. Especially Traverse, who had been through so much, with his big sad eyes, looking at me like, "I know you tried your best, kid. You just weren't up to it." I just wanted to help him sooo much. But it was all turning out like the cats again. I was trying to do the right thing, and I just ended up hurting him. And there he was with his leg and the neat rows of stitches that had been coming along so well — swelled up like a balloon. Just ruined.

Amy must have said something, because Dave came over to me, curled up bawling on the hay-bale-couch. He put his arm around me.

"Sar, I want to tell you something. Sometimes you can be too nice. Horses don't live in a world where a new sweater can make things better. They can't use crutches or wheelchairs. For them, life is a lot harder. If they can't walk, they'll die. We can't spoil them because we feel sorry for them. They depend on us doing what's best and what's right — not what feels good. It's better for them if we face reality. Does that make sense?"

I nodded yes. I was still doing that half-hiccuping thing you do when you've been crying too much.

"You can't just look at the surface of his wound. Matt will tell you. His skin is healed nicely, but underneath all the muscles and tendons need time. Get it?"

"Yeah," I had my voice again.

"What did I say?"

"Face reality. Don't be nice. Look past the surface."

"Right," says Dave.

"Sounds like a good recipe for life," says Matt from where he was applying a cold pack to Traverse's leg.

"She doesn't need a recipe for life right now," Dave answered. "She needs to get this horse healed."

"Hmmph," says Matt — kinda like the way Amy does when Jeff corrects her.

Matt gestured for me to come over to where he was working on Traverse's leg. "Put your hand here," he said.

He placed my hand gently but firmly along the long bone of Traverse's leg. He called it the pastern bone. "What does it feel like?"

"It feels tight, and big."

"Anything else?"

"It's a little warm, but not too much."

"What else?"

I looked at him. I didn't say it, but I thought, "What else could there be?" What I did say was, "What am I looking for?"

Matt said, "That's one of the biggest mistakes people make — to wonder what they're SUPPOSED to be looking for instead of just SEEING. Trust yourself. You know horses — more than you think. What occurs to you? What's the same as it always is? What's different? Ask yourself: 'What am I thinking?'"

It's a really weird experience to have to think, "What am I thinking right now?" But I was still for a second, and it occurred to me.

"My touch doesn't seem to hurt him."

"Good. What does that make you want to do."

"I want to press a little bit and see if a little more pressure hurts him."

"Have at it."

So I pressed around — pretty gently. Traverse just looked at me. He didn't jump or flinch.

"Okay," I said.

"Okay," said Dave, crouching down with Matt and me. "What's your diagnosis, Dr. Sarah?"

"Diagnosis? How am I supposed to know?"

"You just asked all the right questions. You felt the leg. From the looks of things, you've turned this barn in to a dorm room and have been living with this horse. You know him as well as anyone. Ask yourself: what do YOU think?"

Okay, coming up with what I thought this time was much easier than before. When he asked before, it was like prying open an old rusted box that had been at the bottom of the sea for 10 years.

"Well, I don't think anything is hurt or rebroken."

"Why not?" asked Dave.

"Because he doesn't hurt in any specific area when I touch him. Like if I broke my finger and you touched it, I'd go OUCH."

"So what is going on?" asked Matt.

"Well, it seems like walking down the aisle was too much for him and it's like his leg is filled up with fluid."

"Infection?" asked Dave.

"No," I said.

"Why not?" from Matt.

"His leg's not really hot."

"Good," said Matt. "What's your recommendation, Dr. S?"

"I think he needs to stay as still as possible and he should be okay." I thought for a minute. "Can you give him something to make sure if I'm wrong about the infection thing that he won't GET an infection?"

"I already gave him a shot of penicillin," said Matt. "Well," he turned to Traverse, "you are obviously in capable hands."

"Good job," Dave patted me on the back.

I guess, after all, things didn't end too badly. I've been think-ing all night about Matt and the what-am-I-thinking thing. Gosh, it seems like such a simple question, but it's really hard. Do you know, about 90% of the time, I have know idea what I'm thinking?

On the other hand, I always have a crystal clear idea of what Ellie is thinking. Right now, it goes like this: "Get your butt in bed or the stuffed bear gets it."

Nite,

S

📬 To: katie@dundee.net
From: sarah@sarahspage.com
Date: 6-29
Subject: Whose Reality Is It, Anyway?

Hi K,

You know, there are some things I really miss about home. The busy-ness of the city just gives you energy. Someone is always doing SOMETHING. And you feel like you're IN it just cause you're there. Out here I have just too darn much time to think. It's not that I don't like the country, but, as I remarked before, I used the think of the "country" as Westchester County. Lemme tell you. There's country, then there's COUNTRY.

You know when you go out driving — say around Connecticut or Long Island — there are so many trees. And then I swear there's not 200 feet of straight road in the entire Northeast. There's just much more of a sense of — well — closeness. Houses are really close to each other. And towns and villages are really close to each other. You know what Jeff told me: When the east was settled — in the 1600s or something like that — they ended up being just about what you could ride in a day. Isn't that neat? Guess Jeff's a lot smarter than he looks. >:-}

Out here it's not TOTALLY flat, there are some hills, and like I said there are a lot of lakes, but everything is so spread out.

And it seems like there are no trees. Of course there ARE trees, but so much of the land out here is in farmland that the trees just border the fields. They call them "hedgerows." They're kind of neat, too. I like to wander the hedgerows with Ellie. They're all wooded and brambly. Ellie loves it. She's really fast and if she scares up a rabbit, it's goodbye bunny. (Sorry. The blood-lust thing again.) Thing I like about the hedgerows is that they have that closed-in protected feeling. With so much farmland and Michigan being so much flatter than the East, you can feel pretty exposed.

Speaking of exposed, I feel like Matt and Dave unearthed this part of me I would rather had stayed hidden. I keep asking myself, "What do I think?" And "Face reality. Don't be nice. Look beyond the surface."

Well, here's one thing I think: MOST PEOPLE don't live like you and me and the kids we know in New York. And what's more, they DON'T WANT TO. I feel like a big doofus, but all of a sudden I'm realizing: there are lots of people who don't HAVE New York apartments or houses in Southampton and, get this, WOULDN'T WANT TO LIVE THERE ANYWAY. They'd probably think, "Wow. Big, crowded place. Lotta snobs. How lame." On the other hand, around here they probably have their own Southamptons. Only it's someplace you and I would probably think was really lame. AMAZING that people can see the world from such totally different points of view.

So the "What do I think?" stuff has actually brought up some interesting things. The problem is the other part. The "Don't be nice. Face reality. Look beyond the surface."

You know how I've been wondering what's going on with my parents all these weeks. Like, why are they acting so weird? And you and I keep blowing it off and coming up with explanations. Well, here goes facing reality: something IS wrong.

And here's the real kicker: Amy, the one Mom has never been able to get along with, my politically-correct, tree-hugging, liberal, herbal-tea-drinking, bean-sprout-eating, macramé-purse-carrying, tie-dye and sandal-wearing sister is IN ON THE SECRET. Mom has been confiding in her.

There. I said it, and the minute I said it I knew it was more true than ever. The only question is, what do I do now?

Profoundly,

S

✒ To: katie@dundee.net
From: sarah@sarahspage.com
Date: 6-30
Subject: Lack of Communication & Old Books

Kate-o-mation—

You know, I've decided that I'm AWFULLY GOOD at repression. Now that I've decided something really IS wrong at home I DON'T WANT TO KNOW. Weird, huh? I think being a kid is too weird in general, but this kind of freaks me out. Most of the time when you're a kid, it seems, you go around like tell-me-tell-me-tell-me. And the adults won't tell you ANYTHING. When you're really little, they spell things out in front of you. Like, "Don't talk about the P-A-R-K or S-A-R-A-H will want to go." Then, when you learn how to spell, they think they're TOAST. My parents even sunk to the level of speaking pidgin French for a while. Both of them had been sent for summers in Europe to get cultured. When I got into Middle School, one of my teachers asked where I had picked up such terrible French. (I guess neither Mom nor Dad actually GOT cultured in Europe.)

So when they've used up all their secret codes, parents just STOP talking around you. And you go around a lot of the time with this sinking feeling like there's stuff going on but you will never know about it. I guess it's worse when they're arguing, or something has REALLY gone wrong. Then you KNOW something is up, but no one will tell you. So with all the parental repression and not talking about things, I've picked up a really bad habit.

I know I have to ask Amy what's going on, but I just can't stand the thought of it.

I wish Traverse were well so I could start to train him. It's nice, though, going out and brushing him and cleaning his feet and pulling his mane and stuff like that. I've put all that stuff on the Web site, like what brushes I use and how I trim his whiskers and stuff. Gotta tell you, he is the most spiffy looking, spit-and-polish sack of bones you ever saw.

I've been trying to think up some new ways to waste time. Amy tried to get me to join the local 4-H so that I could meet some local kids and hang out. I'm not into it. I'm going to be gone in a couple of months anyway. Why do I want to make new friends HERE? Still, I do end up with a lot of time on my hands. I can't walk anywhere, except to the next field. Occasionally Amy and I drive into town (such as it is), but unless I develop a sudden urge to expand my wardrobe with overalls, the shopping is pretty limited.

I did do some rooting around in the attic. There was a pretty old trunk up there. It had some Laura Ashley-looking wallpaper lining the inside. The paper is really old, so it was probably there before Laura Ashley was invented, but it's the same pretty pattern. It has a lot of old stuff in it like a box of lace handkerchiefs, some old jewelry, and a bunch of old books. I asked Jeff about it. He said it was his great aunt's trunk and that I can do anything I want with the stuff as long as I treat it nice and put it back.

So I hauled out all the books and took them down to my tack room. They're beautiful — leather bound with illustrated plates and tissue paper covering the illustrations and gold on the edges of the pages. And guess what books they are! All the "girl books" we read like years ago. There's *Little Women, Heidi, The Secret Garden, A Little Princess, Anne of Green Gables,* and *The Little House on the Prairie.* Remember, we read all those things — like when we were 8 or 10.

I know you're going to think it's really babyish of me, but I've started in on reading them all again. It's kinda cool knowing that this REALLY OLD WOMAN — I mean, so old she's like DEAD — read these books just like we did years ago. Doesn't that FREAK YOU OUT?

In case you've forgotten, I've put little plot summaries up on the Web. Here's a pop quiz: match the character with the book:

1. Sarah	A. *Heidi*
2. Marilla	B. *Secret Garden*
3. Crotchety Grandfather	C. *Anne of Green Gables*
4. Mary	D. *Little Princess*
5. Pa	E. *Little Women*
6. Jo	F. *Little House*

Later,

S

🖂 To: katie@dundee.net
From: sarah@sarahspage.com
Date: 7-1
Subject: Ingalls Family Values

Hi Kate-astrophe,

I made it through most of *Little House* and *Heidi* yesterday. Well, I guess as far as the Ingalls go, I have to admit the pioneers had it rough. All the details about how they lived and stuff are fascinating. There's that one part — where they've got to cross this river and the kids and Ma are in the covered wagon, which they kind of use as a boat. Do you remember that? Well, for some reason they can't put the dog, Jack, in the covered wagon. He has to SWIM. When they get to the other side and he isn't there, they're all sad. It isn't till they're in camp that night that the poor old dog shows up. Turns out he got swept downstream in the river. Can you IMAGINE?!

Let me tell you: If I went across a raging river in a covered wagon and made Ellie swim, and she finally dragged her butt into camp that night, the first thing she'd do is give me this LOOK then rip up every sock I owned. Like — "Okay, babe. Try walking to the Dakotas without your socks. Think about THAT next time you make me swim."

But of course old Jack just curled up and wagged his tail. Wimp.

Thing about the *Little House* world, though, is that those parental units are so SOLID. They have the solution to EVERYTHING. I guess that's why I enjoyed reading it so much as a kid. Ma is just so LOYAL to Pa, like she trusts everything he does. And cuz SHE does, the KIDS do. And now that I read it again, I have to tell you, I think there are times I would have had that Pa Ingalls' head examined. I mean, they have this nice, cozy house in Wisconsin, but they have to pick up and MOVE because he doesn't like the fact that the neighborhood is getting built up. For crying out loud. It's 1870! Like some DEVELOPER has shown up with plans for a SUBDIVISION called Little House Estates?

But anyway — somebody must've built a log cabin like within 2 miles, so he hauls his wife and kids away in a covered wagon. And where does he relocate them? Ah — you remember! Right in the neighborhood of some pretty hostile Indians. Good going.

Thing is, though, no one in the book ever sees it that way. They're all like, "Yeah, Pa! You really can lead this family." And they just trudge on after him. And, in the end, of course, every cockeyed plan Pa comes up with turns out like the goose that laid the golden egg. So everyone is happy. And they just look UP to him. Like I said, the pioneer details are just great, and it's nice to live in the fantasy world where Pa knows everything, and Ma is sweet and capable and not a bit flaky. On the other hand, I end up thinking things didn't turn out great because Pa was really smart or anything. He was just the luckiest pioneer that ever hauled his keester to North Dakota.

The *Heidi* thing is totally different because it's like in EUROPE — the Swiss Alps. Again, the details are great — especially since I'm now into the animal thing, big time. Those goats! Whatta kick! And that mountain seems like this totally idyllic place. Really Walden-Pond-type stuff. Get away from the hustle-bustle. Chill out. Drink some fresh goat's milk. Pet some nice goats. Great way to spend a summer.

Problem is, once again, I'm just more cynical than I was when I was ten. I mean, it seems like the whole plot can be summed up: unhappy rich girl with serious medical problems (probably all psychological in origin) can find good mental and physical health through fresh air and dairy products on mountain top. Now, not to say that I have actually TRIED the high-altitude, milk-fat remedy. Gotta say, though. I'm not sure it would work for me.

Dave stopped by today. I thought it must be to check on Traverse. But he didn't even ASK to see the horse. I had to offer. I think he was just being sensitive. Like he didn't want me to THINK he had come by to check on the horse. Dave always has on the NICEST clothes — chic jeans and cowboy boots type stuff. Great haircut. Then, too, he NOTICES things around the barn — like the bulletin board I have up of pictures of Traverse. I've also put up some inspirational pictures, like how I would LIKE Traverse to look once this is all over. Dave even admired the job I did on Traverse's mane. Like there's anything ELSE to do with the horse.

So he went into his stall and looked him over, felt around, and did the greatest thing. He asked me again what I thought. I gotta say, "I think he's ready for the next step," is what I told Dave. He said he thought so, too.

So evidently, the next step is to take him out on a lead rope and walk him around. Well, next week Traverse is finally going to be sprung from the Big House!

S

✉ To: katie@dundee.net
From: sarah@sarahspage.com
Date: 7-2
Subject: Little Women & Real Women Do Cut Hay

Katie,

You're right. I know I SHOULD go talk to Amy about Mom and Dad. I feel like I can't right now, though. Maybe I'm just not in the mood to hear any bad news. Or maybe I just want to get a little farther along with Traverse before I deal with anything else that's major. Or maybe I'm still so new at this what-do-I-really-think stuff that I want to practice some more before I have decide what I think about Mom and Dad.

Anyway, my summer reading list is going well. Of course I haven't TOUCHED *Tess of the D'Urbervilles.* I hear you can't even ENTER Mrs. Marcus's room in the fall unless you can like name every character in the book. But I should fit right in with the fourth-grade girls and what they had to read over the summer.

I like Jo March (*Little Women,* in case you forgot) as much the second time around as I did the first. One of the things I can never figure out — and that movie with Winona Ryder didn't help at all either — is: are they RICH or are they POOR? Who the heck knows? They live in this BIG house, and it's obviously in a really GREAT neighborhood because the Lawrences next door have like a ga-ba-jillion dollars. AND they get invited to balls and know what to do. And Aunt March is giving that little brat Amy a full ride to Europe. And yet it's like FOOD and CLOTHING are a REALLY BIG DEAL. And Jo is always talking about how poor they are. For crying out loud, she has to sell her hair to buy a train ticket for her mother. I mean, that's almost like selling your organs or something. So I don't get it. And, once again, why doesn't the father DO something about it. I know he was off fighting the civil war and everything. But, I mean, once he got BACK. Couldn't he get a JOB?

I went back to look at what it says about the dad getting a job. Turns out (I must have read over this before) that he is a teacher and ran a school, but his ideas were so far-out-liberal-PC that the parents totally shut him down. Of course the mother doesn't say, "You LOSER. Get your butt back in that classroom and teach what the parents want you to teach." Instead she and the girls respect him for his principles. Well, I guess the book isn't about the father character anyway. But it's his fault they're all so poor.

Still, I don't get (1) why, if they're so poor, they have a maid and (2) why they don't move to a cheaper house or an 1870-type condo.

My mother has this expression "shabby gentility." She says it comes from England where the gentry — like earls and stuff — inherit these large estates but they're total losers with no skills so they can't get a job and support the place. So the earl just lives in the castle eating gruel while it tumbles down around him. You know, like the grass grows really long and the neighbors complain and stuff. Of course the earl CAN'T move into a condo or anything because he's like an EARL and living in the castle is all part of his whole SELF-CONCEPT thing.

I say, move out of the castle, swallow some Prozac and GET OVER IT.

Speaking of dealing with life head-on, I still can't believe Jo doesn't just marry that rich kid next door and be DONE with it. Of course, she has to follow her heart and marry the professor who doesn't have a penny. If I ever reject a nice, suitable, rich yuppie for some weirdo academic, will you PLEASE DO SOMETHING to stop me? Explain nicely to the yuppie that I suffered a serious head injury as a child and am clearly in need of medical help. Then take me upstairs and like dunk my head in the toilet until I come to my senses. Promise?

Oh — and one more thing. Is it TOO WEIRD or WHAT that the girl character in the book has a boy's name (Jo), and her could-be-boyfriend has a girl's name (Laurie)? Some kinda whacked-out cross-gender message, if you ask me.

Anyway, guess what we have to look forward to next week here at Chez Manure Pile? It's time to cut the hay. I know. I was under the impression that to get hay you call some nice man who arrives with a truck full of hay bales. Then you give him a check and he stacks it nicely in the barn. Turns out, though, that Amy and Jeff are into the bake-your-own-bread, brew-your-own-beer, make-your-own-herbal-tea stuff. So this summer it's bale your own hay!

Evidently, the early summer is the FIRST CUTTING of hay. Have you ever heard the expression "Make hay while the sun shines"? You know — you're at a party and some cute guy is looking at you, and your friend says, "Better make hay while the sun shines," which means, "Get your butt over there and talk to him while he's still interested." Who knew that the expression actually MEANS SOMETHING about hay?

Turns out you HAVE to do the whole hay thing during dry weather because if you bale wet hay it gets all moldy and yucky and the horses won't eat it. AND there's this weird phenomenon where if you bale a bunch of damp hay something chemical happens when the hay is sitting up there under the rafters in the barn. It will SPONTANEOUSLY COMBUST. I know, I know. I thought Jeff was pulling my leg, too. But I actually investigated it. It's TRUE. It's called the "hot hay phenomenon" and I've explained all about it on sarahspage.com.

Type at you later,

S

✉ To: katie@dundee.net
From: sarah@sarahspage.com
Date: 7-3
Subject: Thank God I'm a Country Girl???!!

Katie,

Have I told you that I am in SUCH good shape lately. And I haven't even been able to ride. I owe it all to Ellie. Everything bad you heard about dalmatians when that movie came out is true. She is just so darn HYPER. There's no living with her if she doesn't go on these long walks every day.

When I do take her out, she takes off at like Mach-5. She never runs away, though. She just runs in these huge circles around me. I've been walking so much that I've already worn a path through the fields.

Jeff said that once the corn is higher I won't be able to walk so easily. They have a cornfield in back of the hay field. They rent it out to some local farmer to do whatever it is you do to grow corn. So I'm thinking, cool. I love corn on the cob. Guess what. They tell me you can't eat this corn. Or you wouldn't want to. It's not people corn, It's COW CORN. Who knew cows had their own type of corn? So, they say it's like really dense and really chewy and tastes like flour. YUM. Slap some salt and butter on that stuff!

Anyway, the corn grows like 12 feet high (no kidding). So it's really hard to walk through a cornfield in late summer (duh). Well, I can't imagine how many socks I will lose if I suddenly tell Ellie she can't go on her walks. By now, going on walks and sleeping in the bed are like in her UNION CONTRACT. So I've started to weed up the corn. Yes, you heard me. I'm weeding up the corn. Not the WHOLE FIELD or anything. But a few dozen plants at a time — they're about up to my knees right now — I am creating a path. It should be cool when the corn grows because then the path will be like a tunnel. Oh, and I'm also weeding a big square right in the center — about 8 feet by 8 feet. This will be another cool little clubhouse or fort or something. Take a look at the site — I've drawn out the way it will be when the corn grows. The local farmer will probably think that aliens landed when he goes to harvest. Oh well.

Aren't I getting to be the COUNTRY GIRL?

You know, I guess it isn't really MICHIGAN's fault my house went into the ocean. And it's not Michigan's fault my parents are acting screwy. I pretty much am a New York snob, and I think I'm ALWAYS going to be a snob, but I HAVE learned a lot since I've been here. I haven't MET any of the people — other than Amy's friends — so I can't really say what they're like. I suppose they're just like everybody else — only in a Michigan kind of way. I guess you always feel someplace totally different from your own place is LAME. But I guess that's just a point of view. Weird, you know. This place was so STRANGE when I got here. Everything about it. The really SCARY part is that I don't feel like it's strange anymore.

Remember when we had that exchange student in class and she made that comment about graffiti? She said something like, "Wow, there is SO MUCH graffiti in New York." And you and I and everyone else in the class were like "What? What graffiti?" Okay, so THEN we started to look. Remember? It was like "Once I was blind and now I see." Graffiti was EVERYWHERE. How TOTALLY WEIRD. We're all like, "Wow! There's all this GRAFFITI on all the WALLS. Who knew?" It was all around us, but we totally looked through it. It was like we never saw it before.

Well, I guess I was like that when I came to Michigan. I was like "DIRT ROAD! This is really WEIRD." But, you know, it's getting to be like graffiti. I don't think it's weird anymore. I don't even notice it. And, you know, I don't know whether to be happy or worried about that. Like, will I wake up one day and think that killing cats is okay? I don't know, but at least I'm over the I-can-only-be-Sarah-in-New-York paranoid thing I was feeling before. But now I kind of feel like I'm not being loyal or something — especially to that poor old house. Aren't I supposed to ALWAYS hate it here? Maybe that's stupid.

I'm sorry if I'm not making sense. Sometimes this linear sentence thing is a real bummer. Thank God for the Web.

I'm trying to list on the site all the weird things about living in the country. Check it out.

Later,

S

To: katie@dundee.net
From: sarah@sarahspage.com
Date: 7-4
Subject: Green Horses & Old Roses

Kate-o-rama,

Happy 4th of July! No big display over New York Harbor for me this year, but I AM hearing a lot of small artillery fire from the neighbors' backyards.

Well, tomorrow is Traverse's big day. I'm really concerned about his leg and all. I mean, he hasn't been out of his stall in like FOREVER.

I'm going to take it really slow. Just walk him in one big circle around the pasture then let him eat some grass. I bet he can't wait to eat grass. I mean, can you imagine being a horse and standing in your stall and just LOOKING at all that tender, green, delicious grass but not being able to eat it. And everybody keeps telling you, "Here have some hay." And you're thinking, "Great, just great."

It'd be like you're starving and someone put a big fat hot fudge sundae just out of your reach and said, "You can't have that, but you can have the powdered ice cream we feed to the astronauts on the space shuttle."

YUM. I'd rather eat the cow corn.

I went into his stall tonight and petted his neck and told him about tomorrow. He is still SOOOO skinny. I guess he won't really pork out until he chows down on that grass. I can't wait until he's had his first successful walk. That means that I can actually start WORKING with him. Nothing big at first, just maybe walking him on the lunge line. I've got this great collection of books on how to train a green horse. I've sketched out what I want to do on the site.

So anyway, I went from petting his neck to braiding his mane. I KNOW you only braid a horse's mane for a horse show and all that. But tomorrow is like a really big day, so I thought it was right. I also thought it would make Traverse feel special. But of course he only LOOKED at me like, "My GOD! Get me out of here before she starts with the herbal skin treatments." I must say, I've been so BORED not being able to do anything with him that he is like the most perfectly groomed horse on the face of the earth. The Web site has Sarah's recipe for the perfectly groomed horse. Things like what household products to use, how to condition hooves, that sort of stuff.

BTW2 (aka, Sarah's daily book report) — I think what I like about *The Secret Garden* is that whole secret clubhouse thing. I mean, how cool for a kid to have a place to go that's like a KID place and no one else knows about it. Of course, I've got my tack room and my cornfield. The attic where I found those old books has also become a cool place for me, too. I root around up there whenever I can't think of anything else to do. It's just NEAT having a place of your own where if you want to hang something up you don't have to ASK anyone. It must be like that when you're an adult and you buy a house. It's like the WHOLE THING is your secret clubhouse and you can do whatever you want. How cool.

On the other hand, there's this whole weird morbid thing with that *Secret Garden.* Remember? The garden used to be Mrs.

Craven's special place. And Mary's bringing it back to life. I didn't pick up on the whole resurrection subtext as a kid, and now I think it's pretty weird. I mean, really, you can't bring the past to life. Once it's over, it's OVER. No matter how GREAT the roses looked, once that time is gone, it's gone. I almost think I wouldn't want to BE there constantly being reminded of how it SUCKS that Colin's mother is dead and what a GREAT person she used to be because the garden is SO COOL. But then, as you have mentioned to me on multiple occasions, I am the QUEEN of REPRESSION.

But, I mean, if the old life is dead and gone, wouldn't you rather move on to something totally new? Who needs to make some old roses grow just because they USED to grow? I mean, the new place might not be this totally awesome English garden. Maybe it's just a cornfield, if you know what I mean. But that doesn't mean it can't be totally cool in its own way.

I'll let you know how tomorrow goes.

S

✒ To: katie@dundee.net
From: sarah@sarahspage.com
Date: 7-5
Subject: Knocked Out & Dragged Out

Kate-ophile,

Once again I am flat on my back because of a horse. Only this time it involves stitches and gauze. I'll start from the beginning.

I put Traverse on the lead rope for his first big walk and took him out of the barn. It's real sandy around the barn. Michigan is actually a really sandy state in general. It has to do with the glaciers. Too much to explain here. Go to the Web page if you want to know more.

Anyway, I put the chain over his nose (I wasn't TOTALLY stupid), and I walked him out. My first hint that things weren't going to be completely calm was that his eyes got real HUGE. Like, "Wow, I'm on the other side of the WALL." Then he notices his feet and how they're squishing in the sand. Then he starts to paw. Then he sinks to his knees.

He rolled as if he hadn't been able to roll in years. Horses love to roll (see the site). They do it sometimes several times a day. So he's rolling and groaning and I'm trying to give him enough lead. And I'm thinking. How great. That must feel like THE BEST.

Then this movie starts to play in my head. It's a movie of a horse rolling in a pasture and it's like:

When a horse rolls...
in the pasture...
he rolls...
and rolls...
and rolls...
and then he...
gets up...
shakes off...
and...

RUNS BUCKING AND KICKING AND FARTING TO THE OTHER SIDE OF THE PASTURE.

Only, a horse in the pasture doesn't have SOME IDIOT on the other end of the lead rope.

I realized what was GOING to happen about a nanosecond before it actually did. So Traverse DRAGS me, legs flying, bumping on the ground to the other side of the pasture.

You know, when you're in pony club, they teach you NEVER to wrap the lead rope around your hand. You're supposed to hold the excess in your left hand while you hold the rope with your right. And so you go through pony club constantly being reminded, but never really caring. You do it because you'll get in trouble when you don't. Then when you quit pony club, you stop doing it because you never knew WHY you were doing it in the first place. Well GUESS WHAT? There's a reason.

It's because when your horse drags you to the other end of the pasture on the lead rope and you have the rope wrapped around your hand, it rips your PALM TOTALLY OFF.

I sort of half realized that my palm was ripped to shreds. But I was really more like numb. And my legs couldn't stop shaking, and my heart was pounding so hard I SWEAR Traverse could hear it. And there was this roaring in my ears. And all I could think of was — don't let him see you're afraid. It's really bad to let a horse see you're scared. I'm not really sure why. I only know it's REALLY BAD.

Lucky for me the movie in my head picked up again:

and when the horse...
gets to the other side of the pasture...
he will snort...
let out a big sigh...
and start to quietly eat grass.

Which Traverse did on cue. So at least for the moment I could gather my wits. I took a rag from my pocket and wrapped it around my hand (my left hand luckily). Then I just concentrated on standing up, breathing, not falling down and not crying. I was moderately successful with the standing up and breathing stuff. Traverse was cool. He just continued eating.

I know I shouldn't have been that scared of him. It wasn't his FAULT, after all. Any horse that's been cooped up would've done the same thing. But it was dusk, and standing there, he looked like a huge hooved monster. I was terrified he was going to take off again. And then all I could think of was what COULD have happened. While he was bucking, he could have kicked me in the head. I could have fallen and he could have stepped on me. I could have broken my hand.

My HAND. All of a sudden it started to throb and I realized the rag was soaked with blood. So I thought, Guess it's time to go in.

Man, let me tell you. Putting one foot in front of the other was a real feat. And I'm thinking — Come on Traverse. Please come with me. Because I don't know what I'm going to do if you don't.

Good thing for me he followed me right in with no problems. I think he even scared himself a little bit.

So I went into the house and Amy takes one LOOK at me and goes, "OH MY GOD!"

"Traverse kind of dragged me on the lead rope," I said.

"Get in the car," she said.

So we like MOTORED to the local emergency room. Turns out Jeff was on duty. So Amy like skids to a stop in the nearest parking space and hauls me in by my good arm.

You know, I've never been to an emergency room in Manhattan, which must be a million times worse than one in Reed Lake, Michigan. But, I gotta tell you, what a screwed-up place!

My hand hurt like HELL, and let me tell you it looked like HELL. It looked like my arm had been sucked into a printing press or something because my shirt was totally soaked with blood. So I'm thinking we're going to walk in there and they're going to move into ACTION — doctors running around, hooking me up to monitors, wheeling me away at a dead run.

But NO. I walk in there soaked with blood and they sit us down at this nice registering station and start in with a million questions. They ask Amy to produce a million plastic cards and to fill out a million forms. And I'm thinking what do I have to DO to get SERVICE around here? I swear to GOD, both my eyeballs could have dropped from their sockets and fallen splat on the paperwork and that nurse would have set them aside and continued with the forms.

I can only IMAGINE what it's like to go into a hospital like Montefiore in the Bronx because they must see the most ghastly stuff all the time and not think ANYTHING is an emergency. Too bad if you've got a bone sticking out of your leg. First we've got to help this guy who walked in holding HIS BRAIN in both hands.

Finally, Jeff walked by the waiting room door and saw us. I think he was actually more terrified by Amy's face than he was by my hand.

And WHAT does Amy wail at him? Not, "My poor baby sister! Help her! She's in pain!" No. Instead she wails, "What'll I tell Mom?!"

That's love for you.

So, unwrapping that rag was a trip to the seventh circle of Hell. Amy even went so far as to faint when they were washing the wound. It was pretty grisly, with all the flaps of flesh going everywhere. I nearly passed out, too, from the pain. Then they numbed my hand and Jeff sewed it up. 17 stitches. I'm a regular quilt. Jeff was really cool, though. He calmed Amy down and even joked around with me. He said I'd better be careful with my right hand or else I'll be typing on the computer holding a pencil between my teeth.

So we got home and I HAD to go look at Traverse's leg. It wasn't swollen, so I guess he didn't hurt himself with all that running around. I was feeling pretty gross, so Amy helped me take a bath. Then we both collapsed. She looked like she'd been through the war. I guess she really DOES feel like she's responsible for me, even though we're sisters and we're supposed to be really indifferent and not care about each other at all. She really does. And she's right. Mom would KILL her if anything happened to me.

It's really hard typing with just my right hand. I should go to sleep now. After all, I've been maimed.

S

To: katie@dundee.net
From: sarah@sarahspage.com
Date: 7-5
Subject: Dogs Heal All Wounds

Kate-meister,

I can't sleep. I'm just lying here thinking. You know what's really touching? — Ellie.

When we came home, we could barely open the back door. It was like there was something blocking it — like a rolled-up carpet or something. Actually, it was Ellie. She had her whole body lying up against the back door — like, "Nobody's getting in HERE unless they go through ME." I guess she'd fallen asleep. Then, she wouldn't leave me alone. She always follows me around anyway, but tonight it was intense. While I was taking a bath she was hanging over the tub LOOKING at me. Then she kept lying down at my feet while I was brushing my hair and stuff. I kept tripping over her because she was right THERE all the time.

Then, I tried to go to sleep and she was right there next to me. My hand is all wrapped up in gauze — just my fingers sticking out. It's not dirty any more, because Jeff washed it in the Emergency Room, but the whole hand smells like a hospital because of all the antiseptics and stuff they put on it. So, one by one, Ellie starts to lick my fingers clean.

I know you just want to scream "GROOOOOOSSSSS" and stick your fingers in your ears. Like, "Sarah, you're going to get some WEIRD disease like E-COLI or something if you let the dog do that!" And, yeah, I'm sure the hospital nurse wouldn't have approved. But remember she was the one who didn't care about my eyeballs lying on the desk in front of her. Anyway, all the stitched-up part was under so many layers of gauze Ellie couldn't have gotten to it in a million years. She just very slowly and methodically licked the fingers that were sticking out.

And she was SERIOUS about this job too. I got a little tired of it, so I said, "Thanks, Ellie," and put my hand back under the covers. But she just dove under the covers and started to lick it there. So then I brought it outside the covers, but then she just moved again. THIS time she put one of her paws across my forearm to pin it down. Get this, when I tried to take it back, she GROWLED at me. So, Amy was good enough to put the laptop right on my bed — so I can surf the net and stuff if I wake up. So I just booted it up and let her lick away. When she saw that I wasn't going to struggle anymore, she let out this big sigh like, "Puppies. When will they ever learn?"

Well, I guess in addition to having to face my parents, I have to face Traverse now too. Know what? I'm not really scared. I mean, don't get me wrong, I'm SCARED and all that I'm going to do something wrong and get hurt. But I'm not RE-ALLY SCARED — the way you get when you can't control the situation and you know no matter what you do, bad stuff will probably happen anyway. This time I feel like — well — like Dave and Matt said. No one knows this horse better than I do. And I think he was just playing around and not trying to hurt me. And I think I've learned a lot about horses and how to care for them and how to learn who they are and what their needs are. And I think things WILL go wrong, but I'll be able to figure out what to do. So THAT'S what I mean. Not like things won't be HARD and SCARY, but when they are I have like a CHANCE to DEAL with it.

So THEN there's the Mom and Dad topic. And with that we're back to the can't-control-the-situation-bad-stuff-will-probably-happen-anyway-scenario. Oh well.

I promise. Just let me get through the week, get over the loss of blood, etc. etc. and I will deal with the M&D issue.

Ellie seems to have finished my nightly ablutions. Still won't let the hand go, though. She's got it pinned down like it's her favorite bone and she's sleeping with it.

Nitey-night.

S

✉ To: katie@dundee.net
From: sarah@sarahspage.com
Date: 7-6
Subject: Showdown at the OK Corral

Katie,

I got up. Hand was THROBBING. And I went downstairs to get some coffee. The coffee in this house is GREAT. I mean, it almost makes me get over the fact that there's no Starbucks within walking distance for a quick latte. Jeff's got this OLD percolator coffeepot. It must have belonged to the original settlers. It's kinda gross-looking, you know, with little rusty dents in it and stuff. It's not at all like those yuppie glass coffee makers that everyone has now. You know, the little French jobbies with the plunger that you pay $300 for. This coffeepot is so ugly, I didn't even want to drink the stuff that came out of it. But then I tasted it. YUM. Pioneer Coffee.

Anyway, we were all drinking coffee, and I got some oatmeal and started to put my boots on. Ellie was still guarding my hand pretty intensely. But she was also looking at me like, "Don't think just because I care, you're excused from my walk."

So Amy says, "Sar," She musta got that nickname from Dave, "Aren't you going to take it easy today?"

"Yeah. I guess. I'm just going to walk the dog and take care of the horse. Then I'll lie around." I really didn't feel too bad — once I took some of the painkiller Jeff gave me.

"What do you mean 'take care of the horse'?" You could tell Jeff was trying to stay invisible behind his paper. It's funny how people who aren't even, like, 30 can seem so much like really OLD people. Here Amy is sounding like Mom. And there HE is hiding behind the paper like some 60-year-old guy.

"Where have you been the last few weeks? You know. Feed, hay, brush. Shovel manure. *That's* taking care of the horse.'"

"And walk him."

Wow. Stress. Had to think. "Yeah. I'm going to walk him." You know, if she hadn't turned into MOM all of a sudden, I probably would have said something different, like, told her maybe we should call Dave for help. I mean this wasn't just losing a roll of tape. I'd been wounded. Dave wouldn't have minded. But, of course, I got my PRIDE all involved. So now I HAD to stand my ground.

"I'll use the lunge line, so if he runs off, I can just feed him the line. All I'm going to do is let him eat grass and bring him in. The whole thing will take 20 minutes. I'm doing it this afternoon. THAT'S when we walk." Of course I made that last part up. I could have walked him anytime. But I didn't feel like getting all into this right after I'd had my coffee. Besides, I needed time to think things through.

I've already said that Amy feels arguing is right-wing. So she didn't say anything. Guilt is, of course, extremely PC, so she employs that all the time. She LOOKS at me. Then she LOOKS at Jeff. Her eyeballs must've seared right through that paper, because he put it right down.

"If you want my medical opinion, here it is: her hand's okay as long as she keeps it out of harm's way. If she can shovel manure and walk the horse one-handed, there's no medical reason she can't."

Well, lemme tell ya, Jeff's just lucky Amy's eyeballs CAN'T sear through the paper, because if they could, he would've been a PILE OF ASHES with just this little puff of smoke wafting up. I've already told you what it's like being in the middle of an argument between married people (actually eloped people), so I just skedaddled.

Feeding, grooming, and mucking went well — though it WAS really hard with just my right hand. Then I had a lot of time to think how I was going to work out the walking thing. My spur-of-the moment idea about the lunge line was a really good one. A lunge line is really long — like maybe 16 feet or something. You use it to exercise a horse when you don't want to ride him (see the site). I could use that as the lead rope. I'd hold it PROPERLY this time, and if he ran away, I could just let out the line. Cool.

So, that figured out, I spend the rest of the morning in the attic. You know, Jeff's great aunt's got a TON of cool stuff packed away in that old trunk. I mean, at first you DON'T think it's cool stuff as you go pawing through. At first you think, this is just a bunch of old dusty stuff. But THEN you actually LOOK at some of the stuff. I've described it on the site. For example: there was this BEAUTIFUL lace handkerchief I came across. The lace was totally hand-done. And it had these initials embroidered into it, "IMR." And it was tied up like a little sachet with a little bit of blue ribbon. So of course I had to undo the ribbon. And what's inside? These LOCKS of HAIR. There were 5 separate locks, each tied with a different color ribbon. So HOW COOL. The really eerie part is that you know there's a story behind that somewhere.

Well, the afternoon arrived. I had to keep my word. I gotta tell you, I was REALLY scared. Especially when I looked up and saw that Amy's truck was NOT in the driveway. How could she desert me at a time like this? I mean, who was going to drive me BACK to the hospital?

Well, I DEFINITELY could NOT wait until she got home, because that would say she was right like almost NOTHING else. So out I went. You could tell Ellie was not in support of this plan. While I'm grooming Traverse and stuff, she usually prowls around the barn, looking for mice and sniffing. This time she just lay there like a sphinx looking at me.

Well I groomed every mote of dust out of his coat before I put the lunge line on him. Then we walked out. As we were walking I had this intense conviction that the whole thing was going to happen AGAIN. I just knew it.

And of course it did. Only it wasn't so bad this time. I was prepared. He started to squish in the sand again, and got this I-need-a-fix look in his eyes. So, down on his knees, roll, roll, roll, roll, up, shake and RUN.

But this time he only ran a few strides and gave a half a buck. And with the lunge line, I could bring him right back to me. Then we walked out and he grazed.

It was great to see him grazing in the late afternoon sunshine. He was chowing down on that grass big-time. His coat still looked dull. I guess it's going to be a lot of months before he's in really good health again. I had tucked a book in the back of my pants, so I sat down on the grass in the sunshine and started reading. Now I'm into *Anne of Green Gables.* Cool book. Forgotten how much I'd enjoyed it.

BTW — you know what's awesome about Anne and that whole Avonlea place? First, she's like an orphan and isn't totally screwed up, which proves you can have some really bad experiences as a child and like not end up in prison or an institution or something. She's not perfect — in fact she does really stupid stuff all the time. Which is why I, madam lead-rope-wrapper-around-the-hander, like her a whole lot right now. But the other thing too is that her pseudo-parental units — Marilla and Matthew, who adopt her — aren't totally perfect either. I mean, get this. Marilla makes her wear totally UNCOOL clothes to school because they're practical. Can you IMAGINE your Mom MAKING you dress really stupid, and going to school? I'd DIE. But then the pseudo-parental units realize they're being really dumb and not fair to Anne and they change their minds. So it's this whole you're-not-perfect-we're-not-perfect thing.

So after a few chapters, I decided Traverse had eaten enough. Time to go in.

Remember yesterday I wrote that you're not supposed to EVER let a horse see you're afraid. I couldn't remember why at the time. But now I remember.

It's because when he sees you're scared, he thinks, maybe you're not in charge. Maybe HE'S really in charge. Horses are funny. You'd think they'd know all the time that they could REALLY be in charge if they wanted to. But in a horse's mind it all comes down to one word: ATTITUDE. In a herd of horses, you'd think the biggest and strongest horse would ALWAYS be the boss. But really, it's the horse that has the most attitude that usually is. He goes up to all the other bigger horses and says, "Hey man. This is MY pasture. And if you get out of line, I'll kick your butt." And the other horses go, "Whoa, man. He's got a lot of attitude. He's small, but I bet he could really kick some butt." And that's how they work out their social order. You know — it's kind of like the way New York gangs function.

And if a person strikes the right attitude with a horse, then the PERSON is in charge, no questions asked. And the horses just kind of go around meekly following these little bitty people like, "Man, that human's just a pip-squeak, but what an ATTITUDE." Kinda silly, huh? I mean, horses are SO big, they could like ALWAYS kick your butt. But in their world, it makes sense. I mean the equine with the most attitude is probably the smartest and SHOULD lead the herd. Even if that equine is really a human.

Well, the one thing that really destroys attitude is fear. And in Traverse's eyes my reputation had really taken a beating. So when I asked him to go in, he just looked at me like, "Go away. You bother me."

So then I got more insistent, pulling on the lead. He got irritated and pulled back and stomped his foot like, "Can't you SEE I'm EATING. Now be a nice little human and toddle along." When I tried to make him walk, he just trotted around me in a circle. He REFUSED to go in a straight line, no matter how hard I tried. We just kept on going in these circles and went nowhere. Then he'd stop and eat more grass.

I had absolutely NO IDEA what to do. He was so clearly in charge, and here I was, maimed and helpless. I suppose I could have just unhooked the lead and left him there. But that just felt like FAILURE.

Something inside me told me I couldn't just give up. He was MY horse after all. For years I'd had people present me with TRAINED horses. Okay, so the last one was trained to kill, but still. I'd never had to do it myself. Now I think I realized why fully trained horses cost so much. Because you have to spend WEEKS on something as simple as walking in and out of the barn. Anyway, I KNEW if I gave in, I'd be toast. He'd NEVER do what I wanted, and it would get worse every day.

But here's the MOST FRUSTRATING THING. Horses aren't like dogs. You just can't MAKE them do what you want. They're bigger and stronger than you are. They're kind of like LIFE. You just can't force it to be the way you want. In a brute force match between a person and a horse, the horse will win every time. Unless you, like, get a GUN, but that kind of defeats the whole PET concept. (Been there. Done that.)

So you have only ONE advantage. Supposedly, you're smarter than the horse. Also, horses RARELY lash out. In the wild, they RUN from danger. They're mostly avoidance-type creatures. (Sound familiar? Funny, I'd rather deal with a 1000-lb. beast than my parents. But hey.)

So I started to think about all of this. I thought about something I'd seen at a horse show once. This guy could NOT get his horse to go into the ring. So, instead, he asked people to clear a small area for him OUTSIDE. THEN he REALLY made his horse work. Around and around and around. Finally, the horse was like, "Let me IN that ring. It CAN'T be any more work than THIS."

So what I had to do was make staying outside LESS COOL than coming with me. Well, I couldn't make him work because of the whole broken leg thing. I couldn't make him walk where I wanted. But what I could do was hold his head up and keep him from eating grass.

I pulled his head up, and he looked at me like, "Oh, you again." Then he went back down to eat. But I held the lead tight and braced my arm across my waist. He jerked his nose on the chain. He looked at me, "Oh, come now." He made more attempts and each time yanked the chain across his nose as he went down. I could see him try to work it out in his mind. He was frustrated. He started to circle me on the short lead. I said to myself, "Be a post. If he thinks he's hooked to a post, he'll stop."

And he stopped, and just stood there. He really couldn't DO anything. There wasn't enough lead for him to walk away. He couldn't eat grass. His only option was to just stand there. I was feeling pretty cool. I mean, what I was doing was working so far. At least it was making him think like, "Wait. I thought the boss lady had lost her ATTITUDE."

After a few minutes, I tried again to make him walk nicely to the barn. I think it took him a minute to catch on to what I was doing because he took about 5 steps just perfectly. Then the lightbulb goes off in his head again like, "Hold on a minute..." and he starts to trot around me again. But I was really encouraged. So I made him stop and stand there. And he's like, "Jeez! Not THIS again."

The next time I let him move, I got like 50 feet more before he started to misbehave. Then we went back to standing. By this time, I was getting pretty cocky. So while Traverse was standing there being one frustrated horse, I was just like humming a tune, admiring the trees, and the sky. That's when the toe of the boot in the hayloft caught my eye.

Now, I suppose there are OTHER people in the world who wear purple lizard skin cowboy boots under perfectly pressed Ralph Lauren jeans. But at that moment I couldn't think of anybody but Dave. And I KNEW that behind those purple-lizard toes HAD to be some Amy-canvas-sneaker toes.

They were WATCHING me.

I tried really hard to keep from smiling and really hard to not look for their eyes peering through the cracks in the barn wood. I just kept up with what I was doing. The third time I stopped Traverse was the last. He trotted half a circle, looked at me real bummed like, "Man, this is NO FUN anymore," and just kind of gave up and walked nicely the rest of the way.

Let me tell you. I was SO PROUD of myself. All those years riding but never knowing this whole mystery world of horses. You think you're just not good enough or smart enough to understand. You're just a rich kid who lives in Manhattan and rides on weekends. Actually, the way you feel is kind of like the way you feel being a kid in general. There's this whole adult world that is this big SECRET. And you CAN'T figure it out until you get the adult SECRET DECODER RING. Well, who KNEW? I actually CAN! And the BEST part about it was that DAVE had seen the whole thing.

I was BURSTING by the time we got into the barn. I just yelled out, "Hey DAVE! I like those purple boots!"

So Amy and Dave come thundering down the old barn stairs from the hayloft. Amy just FLIES down the aisle and gives me this HUGE hug. The hug was part — "Wow! I'm glad you're okay" — and part — "Man, my little sister is AWESOME with that horse." After Amy was finished slobbering, I looked up at Dave. He was a few paces behind her with a Marlboro Light elegantly dangling from his fingertips. You're not usually allowed to smoke in a barn, but with Dave it's part of his whole STYLE thing, so you really can't say anything. Anyway, he's grinning and he just gives me this broad, open-armed gesture like — gimme a hug. So I handed off the horse to Amy and gave him a big hug.

He says, "You are just awesome." And I felt like, yeah, I pretty much am.

The expression on Traverse's face was really funny. He was like, "Man it STINKS to be the loser and have everybody gloat." But I could just tell, in his eyes I was Ms. Attitude.

As I was putting Traverse away, Dave kept telling me what was great about what I'd done. That's what's really super about a good teacher. They don't just tell you when you screw up. They tell you when you DON'T screw up and WHY it was totally NOT screwed up.

"I was really worried about you," he said. He looked down at my gauzed-up hand. "And then Traverse started to be such a butt-head. That was a really tough situation."

"Yeah," I said.

"And any really experienced horseperson" (Dave's really PC and says horseperson, not horseman, which is totally cool with me) "would have had trouble figuring out what to do, but I could see those wheels whirring. And you did just the RIGHT thing. You knew you had to face it and figure it out. You had to DEAL with it right there. That's what I like best about you Sar. You take on the challenge and you deal with it. You don't run away. You are going to make some GREAT horseperson some day."

I felt GREAT. We put the horse away. And Amy asked Dave and Matt to come over for dinner to celebrate. I HAD to come up here and tell you as soon as I could. But, you know, all of a sudden as I type this, I don't feel as GREAT as I did before. Dave was all geeked about my dealing with the horse and facing things head-on. What he was saying was right — about the horse stuff — but totally NOT RIGHT about anything else. I guess I really WOULD rather deal with a misbehaving 1000-lb. animal than with the truth about my parents.

So now I know what I'm going to do. I'm going to talk to Amy about Mom and Dad. I'm going to DO IT. I'll write you later and let you know how it goes.

For now,

Sar

📧 To: katie@dundee.net
From: sarah@sarahspage.com
Date: 7-6
Subject: Really Hard

Dear Katie,

I guess writing that e-mail this afternoon took longer than I thought because by the time I had finished and showered for dinner, Dave was back. Matt had some vet emergency, so he couldn't come. And Jeff was on duty, so it was just the three of us.

After we ate dinner, that's when I had to bring it up. I know it was weird wanting to bring it up with Dave there and all. I know you're supposed to be closer to your family than like to anyone else, but sometimes it's easier when there's this really understanding outsider around. It's what therapy must be like. And then, Amy and Dave are so close, part of me felt that he probably knew anyway.

"Amy," I said, "can I ask you a question?"

Amy HAD to know what was coming because she started to look REALLY uncomfortable. But I was maimed and all, and she's supposed to be the adult.

"Sure," she says with this totally false enthusiasm. "What's up?"

I took a deep breath. All of a sudden I had this really stomach-fluttery feeling like when I was first wrapping Traverse's leg. "I want to know what's going on with Mom and Dad. And I KNOW you know."

So Amy gets this really horrified, wide-eyed look and says, "Oh my God."

Then I got really panicky. I had been trying so HARD to avoid the topic and repress the whole thing that I never really gave much thought to what COULD be wrong. All of a sudden all those things came FLOODING into my mind. It was HORRIBLE.

"OH MY GOD," I said jumping up, "Does Mom have CANCER?"

Amy kind of laughed and Dave kind of laughed and said really quickly, "No, Sar. Your Mom doesn't have cancer. Not your Dad either. Everybody's physical health is fine."

So I guess the fact that I had mentioned like almost the WORST thing that could be wrong gave Amy a little perspective. It's like she was thinking, "Well, at least I don't have to tell my baby sister that her mom has cancer."

"Sarah," she starts, "I don't know if you notice it or think about it — because you're around a lot of private-school, New York City kids all the time — but Mom and Dad spend a lot of money."

"Duh," I said. The only possible response.

"I mean, with the private school tuition and the apartment on the Upper East Side and the house in Southampton. Then there's Mom's shopping, and Dad's private club. And the beach club. And the horse." She was starting to ramble.

"Double Duh," I said.

"It all adds up to a lot of money."

"Yeah," I said. "I thought Dad made a lot of money at the publishing company."

"Well, there was that 8 months when he was laid off and had to find another job. And, yeah, he makes good money, but a lot of people make good money and don't have a house in Southampton. And it was GIVEN to them. And then they had to support it...I don't know how to explain this." She was rambling again.

Dave was obviously getting impatient.

"Sarah. Your parents are broke."

"Broke! What do you mean broke!"

"Well, not TOTALLY broke. Just broke enough to not live the life you've all been living," Amy said.

"Amy, you need to start making some sense here. One minute I'm with Mom and Dad in Southampton and we're doing what we always do, and the next minute I'm here and you're telling me they're BROKE?"

"It all started with the hurricane. I think Dad's been holding this in for a long time. You know, they decided to take that house instead of Grandma's money. And Uncle Jim got the money. And we all thought that was a good deal. But I guess no one ever thought that was a really big house. On a lot of property. And it took a lot of money to maintain it. I mean, Sarah, I don't think you and I ever knew how much it cost to have a year-round caretaker looking after the house even if we weren't there."

"Wow," I said.

"And I guess while Grandma was alive, she gave Dad the money to keep us both in private school. So then, when she died, Dad had to do that himself, and the house was just this big burden. So, it's like, for a long time he's been sliding more and more into debt."

Amy took a deep breath.

"So, after the house went into the ocean, I think Dad just broke down. He told Uncle Jim everything. And together they came up with a plan. Dad would take the insurance money and it would be just enough to get them out of debt and to put aside some money for your college — which they haven't done. And then they're going to take a big chunk and put it aside for their retirement — which they REALLY haven't done."

"At least they have a plan," I said.

"But what it means, Sarah, is that there will be no house in Southampton any more. They're going to keep the property because it's been in the family for years. That would kill Dad to have to sell his family's land. He and Uncle Jim agree on that. But unless one of us strikes it rich, there's not going to be any house on it."

"Oh," I said. That really sucked.

Amy took another deep breath. Obviously the worst wasn't over.

"And Dad has made this promise to Mom and Uncle Jim that the family's going to live within his means."

Amy got this posture like she'd just dropped the REAL bombshell, and looked at me for my response. I had NO IDEA what she was talking about.

"Means? What do you mean MEANS? I have no idea what MEANS means."

"What means means is that he won't dip into savings to pay for things. Like his paycheck carries the family month to month. Mom has even considered getting a job."

Mom? Working? Wow, things were bad.

Dave intervened. "Amy, I think you need to get to the point. Tell your sister what it means for HER."

"Okay, okay." Another deep breath. "Your private school does not fall within their means. Neither does your horse. And maybe not even a private college."

I felt like I'd turned to stone.

Dave urged Amy on. "Mom and Dad may even think about moving to a cheaper apartment. Or even moving out of the city. Once they started to think things through, a lot of things came up for debate.

"So, the point is, right now you have a choice, Sarah. New York public schools aren't the worst. They're really different from what you're used to and a little scary. And since we don't know where Mom and Dad will decide to live, we really don't know what school you'd be going to next year. But you can decide to do it and still go to school in New York, or Long Island or New Jersey or wherever they end up. And you'll see all your old friends — on the weekend. Just not every day in class."

"Or."

"Or," Amy looked like she really didn't want to say this because she didn't know what I would say, so she looked at Dave mostly while she talked. "Or you can stay here with us.

It would just be while Mom and Dad decide what to do. I mean it's taking them some time. It's like there's this whole LIFETIME of stuff they've had to really reevaluate. It's going to take more than a couple of months. And the school system here is really good. It's rated really highly and it's small so it'd be more like what you're used to. And maybe after 6 months or so Mom and Dad will have things sorted out and you'll want to go back. But if you didn't that's totally all right with Jeff and me. We really like having you here and want you to stay if you did want to. And if you went to school here, you'd be a resident. So if you wanted to go to U of M, which is a really good state school, you could. Who knows. Mom and Dad aren't really sure they want to deal with the whole New York scene when they have to give up so much. THEY might even end up out here. Dad's talking like all his options are open. Though I really can't imagine the two of them out of New York. But anyway. That's the choice. And it's your choice. And I'll REALLY understand whatever you decide to do. Really I will."

Dave rubbed Amy's shoulders — like, "Good job. I know that was really hard." It WAS really hard for her. I could tell.

But then, things are going to be REALLY HARD for me. I do feel like stone. I can see Amy wants me to stay. And I know how much it took for her to tell me all that. And for her to have dealt with it alone all these weeks without me knowing. And I really loved her for going through all that. It was a lot for her to offer to have me move in. And after all that I have said about Michigan. I mean, I know she's totally afraid that I'll feel forced to stay but be rejecting the life she loves the whole the time. So somehow I thought of something to say.

"Amy. You are the best. It's like the most generous thing in the world for you to want me to live here. I really don't know right now. I really don't. It's just a lot to deal with. I need some time to think."

So I squeezed Dave's hand, smiled at Amy and said, "Thanks guys," and came upstairs.

So, after telling you all this, I know you're going to be totally sad like I am. And really, Katie, I can't think of anything to say. I can hardly write. I really DO feel like stone. So I need to go now.

S

To: katie@dundee.net
From: sarah@sarahspage.com
Date: 7-7
Subject: The End of the World as I Know It?

Katie,

I'm very sad tonight and very confused. I know you must be really sad too, so if reading this is going to totally bum you out — don't. I understand.

I can't believe I made such a fuss about missing THE BEACH and having to come out here for THE SUMMER — that I was so intense over losing the house. I was acting like my WHOLE WORLD had gone away. And the only way I know that it HADN'T then is that it HAS now.

What am I going to do? My whole life has changed. It's really been changed for weeks now, only I didn't know it. Though I probably DID know it, deep down. And whatever happens, things will be different. That is the absolute WORST thing. No matter what I do, things won't be the same. There isn't any choice that lets things be the same.

I'm going to miss you so much. I'm going to miss laughing in English class and being confused together in Trig. Sharing stuff to put in our lockers. Trading dessert at lunch. Swapping bestsellers instead of doing homework. Thinking of weird ways to wear our uniforms. Making up stupid names for the teachers. And EVERYTHING ELSE. I can't even list all the things I will miss. The apartment, school, friends, summers. Everything about every day of my life will be different. There's not enough stuff in the world to replace all the stuff I will lose.

I'm so numb I can't cry. I can't make sense of anything. All I can think is "What am I going to do?" I can't ever imagine being happy again.

Ellie is lying next to me. She's giving me a look like, "At least you've got me." That makes me cry a little. The love of a STUPID animal. At least that doesn't change.

What am I going to do, Katie? Are you feeling the same way? It's SO HARD to find a best friend. Some people NEVER do it. And you and I almost didn't see that we should be friends. Remember that? I don't want to lose my best friend. Is there any way that won't happen?

So I know you're going to say — of course we'll be friends. We'll see each other. We just won't be going to school together. ANYBODY would say that. I want it to MEAN something. Things change. People drift away. So don't SAY it unless you MEAN it.

I'm sorry. I don't mean to yell at you. It's not your fault my family's so screwed up. I suppose I should be mad at Mom and Dad, but I can't do that either. Maybe it's this total loyal daughter thing. Or maybe it's that I knew they did everything because of me. I don't know.

I feel like I have to shut up now. And maybe stay shut up for a few days. Write if you can.

s

✉ To: katie@dundee.net
From: sarah@sarahspage.com
Date: 7-9
Subject: Flora & Fawn-a

Katie,

I know I haven't written for days. I really appreciate you still
e-mailing me. And I REALLY appreciate your not telling me
what you think I should do. I don't know yet. I really don't.
I'm going to talk about something else.

Maybe it was lucky things worked out this way. But like the
day after I last wrote you, Jeff was looking at the weather map
and it showed that in about 4 days it was going to MONSOON
and not stop for a week. That meant the first cutting had to
be like NOW.

Problem was, he's on this special team at the hospital that
rotates to other places. So for this week he had to haul his butt
2 hours away. He expected to have the evenings free to do the
hay thing. But now he didn't.

So that meant Amy and I were on call. That's the lucky part.
Because let me tell you, cutting hay absolutely ABSORBS your
attention. Amy can drive a pretty mean tractor — so we were
all set with that. But being totally maimed physically and now
emotionally, there was some discussion about whether or not
I could hold up my end.

Weird, you know. I was like, LET ME DO IT. And I WANT TO DO THE HAY. Nothing could have kept me away. I think it's because I REALLY needed something to do.

So here's how it works: it's been really dry, hot weather, so the timing is perfect. We'd get up, have our coffee, and wait for the dew to burn off. I'd keep occupied and keep from thinking by doing my chores with Traverse. ("Chores" is a real farmer word that I'm starting to use.) Then we went out to do the cutting. It took us the whole day to cut because the tractor is really old. Amy was the grim reaper on the tractor and I was the scout. This means that she has to (1) drive (2) keep her rows straight. I have to (1) keep looking forward to make sure she doesn't run over a big rock or a stump or anything (2) keep looking backward to make sure her blades haven't been hung up on anything weird, like some old piece of wire or something.

I call her the grim reaper because as far as the little critters (yes, another farmer word, "critters") in the field are concerned, that's exactly what she is. In front of the tractor you can just see the grasshoppers jumping every which way as she approaches. Like, "Oh MY GOD! It's ARMAGEDDON!" Then as you look behind, they're all hopping around on the now-totally-bald field going "MY WORLD! It's DESTROYED." And I'm like, "Yeah, guys. I know how it feels."

The sad part is that sometimes the non-bug critters bite it too. There's the occasional field mouse or even small bunny that can't get out of the way fast enough. I know there isn't any choice and all — like what are we going to do, cut each blade of grass with a scissors? But it's all too close to that whole cat thing. I'm all into Ellie murdering mice when they're in the HOUSE and stuff. Still — on the tractor I felt like an invading army going into their homeland and just pillaging.

There was this one thing that happened that is hard to believe. There's a spot in the field that's kind of marshy. Amy says it's really wet in spring. But we were pretty sure it was dry now. Only thing is we didn't want to be proved wrong by watching Jeff's tractor go GLUG GLUG and disappear into the mud. So Amy asks me if I wouldn't mind walking ahead and making sure the ground was firm.

Now, there are a lot of reasons that a week ago I would have said NO WAY. Reason #1 — I don't want to go Glug Glug and disappear EITHER. Reason #2 — SNAKES!!!!! But somehow, this week I don't care whether I get sucked under by quicksand or bitten by a snake. There's a big part of me that really hopes I do.

So in I went. I started to thrash around and stomp here and there — the grass was up to my shoulders — when I stepped on something soft and heard this loud "WAHHHHHHHHH!"

Well I've pretty much decided that when you step on something soft in Michigan it's probably an animal, so I jump back about a hundred feet. Then I wave at Amy to STOP. So I look down, and there is this TINY little fawn, all snuggled up and LOOKING at me with these big deer eyes. It was SO TINY. Like Ellie is like twice as big as this thing was.

So Amy comes running over.

"Oh My GOD!" she says. "That fawn was just born maybe hours ago."

"How can you tell?"

"It can't get up."

"So the mother deer just LEFT it here?" Animals have this way of doing things that are so COLD sometimes. And you can't be mad because they're animals and that's just the way life is. But there are times when you just want to call Animal Social Services or something.

"Well, yeah. But it's not like it sounds. When fawns are born they have no scent. So the mother will leave the baby in the high grass. Nothing can sniff it out. No wild animals can find it unless they literally stumble over it."

"Like me."

"Yeah. So it seems like this little one is abandoned, but the mama is around here somewhere. Let's not touch her."

Just when Amy said that, Ellie, who'd found us and started sniffing around, goes up to the baby and licks its nose.

And I get this overwhelming sense of — "BAMBI!"

We shooed her away, of course.

"Okay," says Amy, "back to work. We'll just cut very gently around her little world here. She should be able to get up in a few hours. So tonight we'll come out and check to see if her mama came and got her."

So we cut this WIDE circle around the baby deer and went on our way. We felt good that we had given the little thing a chance.

It's horrible to think, but you know it happens that a lot of farmers must just mow right over these little babies. Weird that nature has them be born at first cutting. But, then, I guess nature decided when they would be born before there even WAS a first cutting.

We did go back tonight to check. We waited till after dark, because deer are most active at dusk and we didn't want to interrupt anything. Just as Amy said, the baby was gone.

There was this matted-down place where it had been lying. I suppose now we can go back with the mower.

This is the hardest time of night for me — when there's nothing left to do from the day and all I have left is to think. Sometimes I wish I could just run away from my head. Like, "Here, brain, I don't want to deal with you anymore." It's like there's this big black sad thing inside of me and I don't want to even LOOK at it. As long as I keep busy, I can avoid it. I know I'm going to have to look at it sometime and really deal with it. I just can't right now.

Nite,

S

To: katie@dundee.net
From: sarah@sarahspage.com
Date: 7-10
Subject: Princess? I Don't Think So.

Katie,

Today we turned the hay. That's when you go out and use this — well I don't know — it's a hay-flipper-thing you drag behind the tractor. It sort of fluffs up all the rows of mown hay and flips them over so they dry on the other side. We did that today.

Ellie has gotten tired of running beside the tractor. So now she just sits at the highest point in the field and watches us. Kind of like the foreman — uh, forewoman. I can just feel her saying, "Work, girls! Work."

So, it's totally ironic that I saved A *Little Princess* book for last. Yeah, I know. WEIRD.

A refresher: They're British, and it's WWI. Her father, who has like a ga-jillion dollars, puts her in a New York boarding school while he goes off to war. I read somewhere that a lot of rich people during both WWI and WWII sent their kids away to the U.S. to keep them from being bombed off the face of the earth. So then the father DIES (but not really) and the British government seizes all his assets (I don't get why) and Sarah (don't even MAKE the comment) is toast. The totally evil headmistress makes her be a scullery maid. (What IS a scullery? Why does it need a maid?) And she has to live in the attic with the rats. And there's this little black kid who's her friend and is like the nicest kid in the world.

And the part that TOTALLY SUCKS is that at the end of the book, it turns out her father wasn't really dead. He just lost his memory. (How many times have we seen THAT in a movie?) And he comes back and Sarah is rich again and the dad totally kicks the evil headmistress's butt. Get REAL. Like that EVER HAPPENS.

So I was ready to throw the book in the manure pile. The only thing that keeps me from doing it is that Sarah has this really terrific imagination. And that part of the book is as cool as it ever was. She can imagine ANYTHING and it's real to her. It's so real that she gets the little black kid totally into it. Then all the rest of the kids in the boarding school (who are these completely snobby New York rich kids who diss Sarah entirely when she loses all her money) want to be her friend again because she tells these STORIES. And she makes everybody get INTO it. It's like they can feel, and hear, and smell what she imagines. And throughout the whole book you get this sense that her imagination is this really good thing. I mean, they could have made it sound like she was totally delusional or something. But it's not like that at all.

Remember when I first came out here and I wrote you about being sad. That was when I was sad about stupid stuff. Not like NOW when I really have something to be sad about. I remember saying that I thought the Web site was stupid and all this e-mail is stupid and that bytes on a chip are more important to me than the real world. I made like it was really lame.

I was wrong. I mean, this is MY WORLD. And it IS real, even if it is only bytes on a chip. Who's to say that the real world is any REALER. Look at the old-guard world my parents lived in. You'd think that was real. You could smell it and touch it. Other people were there. But that, like, went out with the tide (pretty much literally). So I'm not going to diss my computer world anymore. It's real. It's a world. I live in it. And the site. I made it. It's mine. It's a lot more than just words. It's sounds, and pictures. You can reach me, I can reach you. The only thing you can't do is smell through the computer. But who knows? Technology is advancing every day. On the other hand, since the main odor around here is manure, it's probably good there is not smell support on the Internet. What would they call that streaming technology anyway? RealAroma?

For a while now I've been regretting being born when I was, instead of, say, when Amy was born. Because if I was born then, there would still be money. But I guess there are advantages to being born when we were because of the whole TECHNOLOGY thing. We can create this new world and BE in it. I don't know. Maybe I should have my head examined, saying that world on the screen inside the Internet is real in its own way. But I guess I'm just like that other Sarah. It's real to me. I'm happy here. So beyond that, I guess nothing much matters.

Wow. I've gotten pretty deep. But these thoughts make me feel good. I'm going to try to hang on to the good feeling and go to sleep now.

S

From: sarah@sarahspage.com
Date: 7-11
Subject: New Levels of Physical Pain Wipe Out Mental
            Anguish

Katie!

I'm exhausted! Today we baled. Now THAT's work.

Remember that day we walked from school to Canal Street? Remember how tired we were? Must have been like 6 miles. I'm telling you that's NOTHING compared to baling hay. Those pioneers must have looked like they spent HOURS on the Stairmaster. Just think about it. They did what I just did to-day, and that was, like, only their MORNING. THEN they went out and dragged a bunch of rocks out of a field, or chopped wood or something.

Amy drove the tractor, but this time she pulled something entirely different behind it. It's like there is NO LIMIT to the number of things you can drag behind a tractor. Today, she pulled the baler. The baler has these blades that scoop up the hay and shove it through this channel that makes it into bales. Then there's this sewing machine part of the baler that ties string around the bales. The bales come out the back on this conveyor-belt thing. On top of the baler is the kicker (yes, the kicker) that pops the bales up and into the hay wagon that's behind the baler.

My job was to walk alongside the baler to make sure the thing didn't get clogged up or anything. If it did, I'd have to run up to where Amy was driving, so she could HEAR me over the tractor and tell her to stop. Then we'd wrestle with the baler. Then we'd start again. Running alongside that baler in that field in the hot sun sure took it out of me. But THAT wasn't even the hard part.

The hard part was unloading the %$#^%&^& hay wagon. We used these long hooks that you stick into the bales. It took two of us to carry each bale. We'd climb into the wagon, spear it with the hook, then climb down and haul it into the top level of the barn. We'd shimmy it over next to all the other bales and do it again.

I guess after a while, we just started to feel like machines ourselves. The sweat's dripping down your face and back, your legs are pumping, and you just keep going with this weird cosmic oscillation. Like the hay, and our bodies and the whole, sunny, critter-filled world was just one buzzing, beating, breathing, working THING. Amy and I didn't even have to talk to each other to stay in rhythm. We both just DID because we were so INTO what we were doing. We even stopped counting one-two-three-THROW to throw the bales on top of each other. We just KNEW when to throw. You know we're almost in the year 2000 and we forget that at one time people and animals WERE almost the only machines. Like if this were 100 years ago, Traverse would be out here pulling the hay wagon and Amy and I would be swinging scythes. But even WITH machines, it's pretty rough work. Our arms and hands got all scratched up because dry hay is really sharp stuff. And there were all these little bits of hay stuck to the sweat on our faces. We finished 100 bales with 100 more to go tomorrow.

Like I said before, I'm really glad to be doing this work. It's so totally absorbing, that it takes away the sadness. I could even HANDLE talking to Mom, if you can believe it.

Amy and I came in, just WIPED, and SAT down at the dining room table. It's like we couldn't even move to take a shower. We were THAT tired. So the PHONE rings. Each of us looks up as if we'd just been asked to climb Mt. Everest. Getting to the phone was a really big deal. I eventually got up, and it was Mom on the other end.

I knew from her "How ARE you, sweetie?" that she knows that I know, and she and Dad are every bit as sad and torn up about this whole mess as I am. And while I really HAVE been angry at them for taking my life away, I know it's not their fault. Well — it kinda is. They're the adults and I guess they didn't make the best decisions along the way. But then I AM the one who got dragged through a field at the end of a lead rope, so, like, what room have I got to talk? And then I feel like there are times when you TRY to do the right thing but there's this STUFF in the way called LIFE. And you can't change it. And you end up feeling like you've done the WRONG thing, even though you didn't know what else to do. Like with the cats.

And we're talking about Mom and Dad's life, too, after all. They've got it worse, because they have to worry about how it will affect me — especially when my mom's convinced I tried to commit suicide ONCE already. So I guess after taking all that into consideration, I really am NOT that mad after all. What good does getting mad do? It doesn't change anything. I feel really bad for them and I don't want them to feel guilty about me. So I told my mom I was JUST FINE and that I was pretty happy (lie) and I thought I could make a decision on school pretty soon (double lie).

It made me feel good just to talk to her. We've kind of been avoiding each other all summer. So then Amy and I took showers and lay down on the floor in the living room to watch TV. That was about 6 hours ago. We both fell asleep. Jeff woke us up when he came in from work at 10 p.m.

THEN we had to take some MAJOR doses of Motrin because EVERYTHING hurts, including the sunburn. Just think about it. The pioneers didn't even have sunblock, which we were both wearing in MAJOR amounts.

Have to do it all over again tomorrow,

S

To: katie@dundee.net
From: sarah@sarahspage.com
Date: 7-12
Subject: Too Exhausted for Clever Subjects

K-

Last 100 done. Too tired to talk. Hope Traverse appreciates all this. Ellie looking like, "Man, you gotta call your union steward or something. This CAN'T be in your contract."

Nite,

S

✉ To: katie@dundee.net
From: sarah@sarahspage.com
Date: 7-13
Subject: Substandard is in the Eyes of the Beholder

Hi Katie,

I feel like I've been hit by a truck. But it is SUCH a good feeling to know that we have all the hay done.

It must have been all the exercise, but I had this WEIRD dream last night. I dreamt that Ellie and I were in Manhattan. And I was really anxious to get back home. Only HOME was HERE. But Ellie would NOT come until I had shown her all the sights and we had collected souvenirs from all these places. It was WILD. I had to take her shopping, and to Central Park, and the Statue of Liberty, to a Jazz club in the Village, and for a ride on the Subway. Man! Finally, we made it back.

It's amazing how much my perspective has changed in the last few weeks. I don't even know how to describe it. It, like, comes in waves. Like today I've been feeling really bad about how snobby I was when I first came out here — to Amy and to everyone else. I never SAID much to Amy — except that one time. But she must have known from the way I acted that I thought this place was completely SUB-STANDARD. You know, when you could end up ANYWHERE it seems like you have no right to be snobby about ANYPLACE. If you were in a wagon headed west and you said, "BOY I will NEVER live in WISCONSIN. How LAME"! But then you get there and discover that (A) You're really tired and you DON'T want to go to Utah and (B) YOUR 40 acres and a mule happen to be in Wisconsin. So who's lame?

I guess the really scary part is that when I think about staying here (yes, I DO think about it) the people here might just get really snobby about ME. I mean if I thought THEIR world was really under par, imagine how they would feel about MINE. They'll probably think I talk funny and use funny words. And the more I think how AWFUL it would be if they felt this way and how much I would TOTALLY disrespect them for being so narrow-minded, the more I realize that I have been EXACTLY the same way. So what can I expect?

And it's not just staying HERE that makes me afraid of people like that. You KNOW how it would be in some public school or some parochial school in New Jersey or something. They'd be like, "So where did you go to school last year?" And I'd tell them, and they'd know it was a private school in Manhattan. And they'd be like, "So you must think you're better than us. We don't want to talk to YOU."

I don't feel like I'm better than ANYONE right now.

This must be what it feels like to find religion or something like that. The way you used to look at the world is totally defunct and you just can't look at life the same way even if you wanted to. I guess, puberty's kind of the same phenomenon if you want to look at it that way, too.

Am I deep these days, or what?

Amy and I did this totally STUPID thing this afternoon. I went out to the hayloft just to SMELL the hay. You know, like when you paint something and have to stand back and admire it. Well, that's how I felt. It's amazing that we two girls put up ALL that hay. But despite MASSIVE doses of Motrin, my muscles still hurt like HELL. So I didn't want to STAND there and admire the hay. I just climbed up a level or two. (We stairstepped the bales as we stacked them so you can climb to the top.) And then I lay down. It was hot and sweet smelling. Just the way you'd expect a hayloft to be in July. So I'm just lying there thinking about all the stuff I just told you about, maybe snoozing some, and Amy comes in. I guess she had the same urge that I did. So she climbs up on the bales and lies like three bales away. So there we were, the two of us, lying there like a couple of doofus-butts. We lay. And we lay. I guess she dozed. I know I did.

So Amy, who can't let a perfectly good corny moment alone, says, "I'm going to miss you when you go back to New York, Sarah."

I couldn't help myself. I just sat up and said, like a total idiot, "Who says I'm going back to New York?"

I'm sorry. She caught me off guard. I didn't MEAN it THAT way, like I've DECIDED to stay or anything. It's just that I've been shuffled around SO much lately, totally without my choice at all. It just really rubbed me the wrong way that anybody would ASSUME I was going anywhere. But, of course, you know that's not the way Amy took it.

So all of a sudden she looks up and gets this BIG smile on her face.

So I have to say, "That doesn't mean I AM staying Amy. It just means that I haven't decided yet."

"But you can't deny that staying IS an option?"

Man, she should have gone to law school. "Yes. I can't deny that staying is one of my options."

So I totally blew it. Cuz she gets up all smiles and like goes humming into the house. Now she'll get her hopes up that I'm going to stay. And she'll do that twist-your-words-against-you thing that PC people ALWAYS do. If I decide to go back, she'll say, "But you SAID you were going to stay!"

Katie, I'm serious here. I'm not asking for you to give your opinion because I KNOW when this first happened you said you would DEFINITELY NEVER do that. But I'd like to know what you think about how we can stay friends. I mean, if Mom and Dad decide to move to New Jersey or Long Island or something, it's still going to be way difficult to see each other. Maybe just as difficult as if I stay out here in pioneer-land. I'm not looking for the prick-your-finger-and-swear-in-blood-that-we'll-always-be-friends type thing. I'm looking for PRACTICAL ACTION STEPS. What are we going to DO?

So I'll come up with some ideas, too. Then we'll make a list.

Later,

S

To: katie@dundee.net
From: sarah@sarahspage.com
Date: 7-14
Subject: Mr. T & Action Steps

K—

I haven't brought you up to date on the horse in a while. So I thought I'd better.

After that whole triumph-in-front-of-Amy-and-Dave thing, (you know, right when my life fell apart), I kept working him on the basics — walking on the lead rope.

It's AMAZING how much work goes into just getting a horse to walk on the lead rope properly. He's supposed to walk RIGHT next to you, and not drag you around even a little bit. So you have to put the chain over his nose, and if he starts to tug you along, you give it a yank. And you carry a whip so if he starts to dawdle or won't go somewhere, you give him a thwack.

Then, you have to get him to back up on the lead rope. I've seen a lot of people getting their horses to back up by putting their shoulder up against the horse's chest and shoving backward. Very subtle. REALLY the right way to do it is to give a short backward yank on the chain and say, "Back." If he doesn't, then you tap just below his knees with the whip. It's kind of funny because the horse is like, "Hey, ouch, that hurts. Cut that out," as he lifts up one leg after another and moves away until he's actually backing up. The next time you say, "Back" he does this whole, "Wait. I remember this," and backs on his own.

So Traverse and I are just champs at walking around with him on the lead rope. He's even graduated to short spans of time out in the pasture, which he LOVES. So, basically what I'm saying is that I have a perfectly behaved 1000-lb. dog. Leash trained. Stays in the yard. Lovely.

Naturally, the key problem with this is that he's a HORSE. I HAVE put him on the lunge line a couple of times. He just walks around me. No trotting yet. It's not allowed. So he just walks with this really disgusted look, "How much FUN can one horse take?"

So today I called Dave about the what's-next issue. He says since I don't weigh much (bless him) that I could get on him and take him for short walks around the pasture. YIKES! Luckily Dave said he wants to BE there for the first time I get on. He says he wants to watch from the ground for any sign of soreness. Total liar. He wants to make sure I'm okay. It's the old don't-let-a-16-year-old-get-up-on-a-racehorse-by-herself thing. I tell you. Adults and their overprotectiveness. (Double-bless him.) He's coming tomorrow.

So, if you merge your list of how-we-stay-friends steps and mine and eliminate the totally stupid stuff (like your parents would ACTUALLY agree to adopt me), we get the following:

ACTION STEPS KATIE AND SARAH CAN USE TO STAY FRIENDS EVEN IF SARAH LIVES WEST OF THE HUDSON

1. e-mail
2. e-mail
3. e-mail

4. e-mail
5. Katie comes to visit Sarah twice a year (summer and winter break)
6. Sarah comes to visit Katie twice a year (Christmas and Spring break)
7. Sarah and Katie use the Web site for a multimedia experience of each other's lives
8. Sarah and Katie apply to (mostly) the same colleges
9. Sarah and Katie agree to involve each other with their OTHER friends. Example: We say things like, "My friend Katie from New York would know just what to do here. Why don't we e-mail her?"
10. We prick our fingers and swear in blood that we will stay friends.

So, I think that's a pretty workable list. Don't you? Something we can totally live with.

S

To: katie@dundee.net
From: sarah@sarahspage.com
Date: 7-15
Subject: Back in the Saddle

Kate,

I think Ellie knows what's going on. The last couple of days when she kills a mouse she's been bringing it to me and laying it at my feet. Like, "If you stay here, I'll share my mice with you." YUM. Hard to turn down an offer like that.

So I rode the horse today. I wish I was a good enough writer to tell you just how important a thing it was. Everything from putting the saddle and bridle on. Things I've done a ba-jillion times before, and yet I felt like I was learning how to buckle each buckle for the first time. It felt like slow motion.

So then, he was all set. Saddle and bridle and everything. And I had my riding gloves on, the same ones I had on when I took my swan dive. And like Dave and I both KNOW that it's a big deal for Traverse, too. Because the last time he had someone ride him wasn't the most totally positive experience for him EITHER. So Traverse and I are looking at each other like, "So, did you take your Prozac this morning?" And Dave and I both knew it was completely possible that (1) I would get on and totally not be up to it and have to get off or (2) Traverse would totally spazz out, like "I remember this deal. The next thing that happens is I BREAK MY LEG."

Traverse is really tall, so Dave just pulled over a hay bale and I stood on it to get on. He held Traverse real still. I did it as slowly and as gently as I POSSIBLY could. I put my foot in the stirrup and I just stood there for a minute. Then I rested my hands on the crest of his mane and put all my weight there and in the stirrup. Then I slowly swung my other leg over and REALLY SLOWLY straightened myself till I was sitting up. I think it was only then that I started to breathe again.

Dave and I looked at each other. Okay so far. I patted Traverse's neck. Dave let go of the reins.

"You're on your own, babe," he said.

I looked down at Traverse who looked back at me like, "You're cool, I'm cool. I won't break your head if you don't break my leg." So I gave a gentle cluck and he stepped forward.

KATIE — I can't TELL you how COOL it was to be sitting on his tall, tall back stepping on the leg that I helped him heal. And I was just sucking in the grass-smelling air and taking in the view. And we were WALKING around the pasture. And I was RIDING MY HORSE. And I turned him to the right to go around the tree, and we WENT AROUND THE TREE. And we were okay.

Amazing that just two months ago I was swinging into the show ring to jump 3-foot fences. Walking around on a horse was something I totally took for granted. And now walking this horse around the pasture was a WAY BIG DEAL. I can't explain it. All I can say it that all of a sudden it was a much bigger accomplishment than jumping 5 feet at the Olympics. It just WAS. WE WERE WALKING!

The deal with Dave was I could only ride 5 minutes the first day. Dave would keep time. Then day by day I'd work Traverse up, maybe adding a minute each day. After a week or so I could trot. So Dave yelled time, and I got off. Dave gave me this BIG hug and we walked to the barn together. I know Dave has rehabbed a TON of thoroughbreds. I really appreciate that he understood what a big deal this all was for me.

So we put the horse away. And then I got this big urge to talk to Dave. I guess I was feeling emotional. But I HAVE been wondering about Dave and his lifestyle for quite a long time. Funny. I just felt so comfortable that I started asking him questions. I didn't even think, "Boy, how RUDE." I just started to ask him how it was that he was cool living out here, and didn't he feel totally out of place and why didn't he go somewhere like New York or San Francisco or something.

"I'm sorry," I said. "I like didn't even ask you if it was okay to talk to you about this."

"No," he said. "It's cool. It's just it's hard to answer your questions. I've never thought about living anywhere else. Not that I couldn't."

I gave him a look like "I don't get it."

He said, "I guess I could tell you 'this is my home.' And I think when I was 17, I probably would have said that. Like, this is my home and you're not going to make me leave it. But, I mean let's get something straight, Sar. Just because the people out here don't live in New York or San Francisco doesn't mean they're closed-minded about people like me. Some of them are. And some of them aren't, just like anywhere."

"But, Dave. I mean, you're telling life wouldn't be EASIER for you in the Village?"

"Yeah, I guess in some ways it would be easier. But, I mean is that the point? Having it be easier?"

He had me there.

"Look, Sar. Home isn't this PLACE that's completely designed so that you are comfortable. Home is something else. In many ways, it doesn't have anything to do with a place at all. It's who you are and what you carry with you and how cool you are with that. I'm here because I like it here, and I can be me here and there's no reason to leave. My horses, my farm, my life. It's ME. You'll never be at home anywhere until you're cool with yourself — no matter how good or how rotten the people around you treat you."

Then he got up.

"Wait," he said. "I want you to hear something."

So he gets up and runs out to his truck and comes back with a guitar. Who knew Dave played the guitar? So I think he's going to start playing "Cumbaya" or something. But instead, he starts picking really lightly on the strings. It sounded pretty, sort of Celtic. And then the little harp-bell picking turned into a tune and I was pretty sure it was Celtic. And then in this really soft voice he like sings this sad song. I guess you'd call it a lament. It was about a sailor or something. And it was all like — "It's really sad to leave my home, but I have to go, and I'll carry my home with me and it'll be better because it'll be in my heart all the time."

So, how do you reply to THAT? But in a funny way, I really GOT IT. I will HAVE to MAKE Dave record the song for me. He promised he would. Then you can hear it on the site. There's no way to describe it. Once I heard it, I just UNDERSTOOD.

I guess what I GOT is that HOME is the sum of experiences — both in time and in place, that travel with you and make you YOU. It's like the settlers coming over to the New World, or

Jews or Gypsies or people in covered wagons that traveled west carrying all the things that made up their lives with them. Sure they loved the place they left, and that place would always be their hometown or homeland or whatever. But the HOME thing was more of a portable concept to them. It was IN them, not a thing they left behind.

And I guess you can miss your homeland, just like you can miss being 8 or 10 years old or whatever. But you can never go back there again. First because it's impossible, and second because IT changes and wasn't what it was before, and YOU change and weren't what YOU were before. What you really long for is just an idea, a memory, and can't be real again.

Actually, it's not as sad as it sounds because that memory thing is really strong. It's like you can have all the NEW-world stuff of NOW and all the OLD-world stuff of THEN at the same time. You know, like e-mail. It isn't totally NEW. It uses WORDS and all, and they were practically invented by the caveman, or homo-whatever-you-call-him. And e-mail uses punctuation, which is old. Though some things are new :-) same with the site — it has music, and pictures. Old ideas, only now they're clickable.

Don't be sad, Katie, but I think what I'm trying to say, is that I'm going to STAY. Going back to New York would be like trying to un-invent something that has been invented, or un-discover something that has been discovered. It's like I don't want to be some guy sitting in a cabin in the woods because someone invented the telephone and I've decided I HATE the telephone. It would probably just be easier to get caller ID.

You're my best friend, Katie. And thousands of e-mail words later, you're better than my best friend. Amy is my sister and all. And how can you be more than a sister? Well I guess you really can. And YOU really ARE. I know I don't have to explain. That's the amazing thing. I know you GET me and what I feel. And you DO UNDERSTAND. But I don't want to take that for granted. I'm a smart-aleck. And you don't care because you always know what I mean. But that's not enough right now because this is a really big deal. I have to say it.

Thanks, for being my friend, and for promising to STAY my friend, even with me here — and for GETTING IT, always, about me.

Love,

Sarah

Author Biography

Like Sarah, **Anna Murray** is a transplanted New Yorker.
Born in Southampton, Long Island, she lived most
of her life in and around New York City.
Now she lives on a farm in Michigan
with her husband Jim, her horse, Sutton's Bay,
and two Dalmatians, Ellie and Cleo.
In 1997 Anna started her own Internet company
that designs web sites, such as the
home of the Keebler Elves.